Loose
ENDS

Loose ENDS

A NOVEL

NEAL BOWERS

RANDOM HOUSE NEW YORK

RANDOM HOUSE and colophon are registered trademarks of Random
House, Inc.

Library of Congress Cataloging-in-Publication Data

Bowers, Neal.
Loose ends : a novel / Neal Bowers.
    p.   cm.
ISBN 0-375-50499-0 (hardcover)
1. Mothers—Death—Fiction. 2. College teachers—Fiction. I. Title.
PS3552.O8732 L6   2001
813'.54—dc21   00-034166

Random House website address: www.atrandom.com
Printed in the United States of America on acid-free paper
9 8 7 6 5 4 3 2
First Edition
Text design by Meryl Sussman Levavi/Digitext

FOR NANCY,
WITHOUT WHOM I WOULD BE AT LOOSE ENDS

Loose
ENDS

CHAPTER 1

THE SHORTEST DISTANCE between two people is almost always a lie. Compared to the truth, it has the advantages of a cut flower over a potted plant. You may think you would prefer the plant, but consider the commitment—the watering, the worrying. You can't help expecting it to live; and if it doesn't, you bear most of the blame. A single rose, however, lasts as long as it lasts in its slender vase. Snip the stem on the bias and cloud the water with an aspirin, but still you know this momentary effusion will not become part of your permanent decor.

Davis Banks lived by this philosophy and always traveled with his arms full of flowers—a daisy for the ticket agent, a jonquil for the steward, and for the person seated next to him, an exotic bouquet.

"Yes, I'm the inventor of the mobile bowling alley. You don't see them much in this country, but they're the rage in Latin America. All you need is a pickup truck, a few sections of my patented collapsible trestles for an extension, my simulated polyurethane lane, and you're in business. Just drive from town to town and rake in the dough."

Such stories illuminated the daily trench, flashed in dull eyes. And Davis especially liked it when one of his original lies came back to him, like the one about the Barber-in-a-Helmet: simply strap it on, set it for the length of hair you want, and flip the switch. But it distressed him when some of his inventions—the Bug Zapper, for instance—became real. It wasn't that he regretted not getting the patent and making a gazillion dollars; rather, he felt disoriented, like waking in a hotel room and thinking for a moment he was in his own home. The truth, too, can be a mimic. Sometimes it dims and blinks, a bulb about to blow.

Studying and teaching literature for fifteen years had conditioned Davis to regard everything as subject to multiple interpretations. Struggling to get his students to understand a poem or a story in a certain way had failed, so he gave himself over to their assorted misreadings, accepting them all as valid.

His own life reinforced this approach. Moving from one teaching job to another, he had settled in finally as an academic oddity at a junior college in Des Moines. His actual title was Part-time, Temporary, Adjunct, Visiting Assistant Professor, his professional identity so qualified that he felt edited almost to invisibility. Of course, he pretended he was full-time and tenured. What did the words mean, after all? Even the world is a text, infinitely interpretable. Self-image is yet another possible version among many, the lie a person tells himself, the fiction of identity.

On this trip, Davis Banks introduced himself as Ben Blau to the man strapped into the seat beside him. He liked names that teased, just for the extra risk. Calculating that his chance companion knew no German, Davis said, "Hi, I'm Ben Blau," which in English/German hybrid announced that he was drunk. No recognition, just an extended hand and a name, "Jim Timmerman," which caused Davis to study hard for a moment. Something in the rhyme sounded concocted. Could be a fellow changeling. Surely there were others like himself, probably thousands; but Davis couldn't say for certain he had ever encountered one. As a test, he allowed Timmerman the first move: "What do you do, Jim?"

"As little as possible." A snorting laugh punctuated the man's answer.

Davis waited. "Good work if you can get it," he said with a guarded smile.

"Actually, I'm a motivational speaker." From his inside coat pocket, he dealt Davis a business card embossed with a blue eagle and the words in red: JIM TIMMERMAN, WINNER OF THE CONGRESSIONAL MEDAL OF HONOR.

Davis was momentarily speechless. This man might be one he could learn from, a big-leaguer going for the long ball on every swing.

"I talk to business groups, civic organizations. You know, pump 'em up and get 'em excited about life. It's a pretty damned good life, after all."

Was the ambiguity intended? Life with a capital "L," or lowercase, as in life as a scam? Davis felt himself wobble with the lift and sway of the plane as he sat transfixed by the card. Why tell a lie that defied belief? Weren't most Medals of Honor awarded to soldiers killed in action, their bravery transcending life? Davis had always specialized in the lie that could be true, that couldn't finally be disproved. But here was a man who had lifted the game to another level, pushing harder on credibility and taking greater risks.

"Sorry, I'm all out of cards right now. Gave my last one to"—he almost said the pope—"the postmaster. In Des Moines. I represent a line of satchels called the Compressor Carrier. It has special compartments for letters. Squeezes the air out of them. Amazing how many more letters you can carry when the air isn't taking up all that space."

"Can you sell independently to local post offices? Don't you need a government contract for something like that?"

Now Davis was even more certain Timmerman was a player. "You're right. I'm drumming up support for my carrier before making application. You know, looking for ways to improve it, trying to generate some grassroots enthusiasm. Can't take anything for granted where the feds are concerned."

Davis was about to pocket Timmerman's card when the other man reached for it. "Sorry. I'm running low, too. In fact, that's my last one, and I'm using it just as a loaner until I get a new shipment."

"So, what branch of the service were you in?" Davis asked, tugging at the knees of his pants and shifting in his seat.

"Marines."

"How'd you win the medal?"

Timmerman's face turned serious, and he cleared his throat as if he were about to address everyone on the plane, then lifted a hand that might stop traffic or swear to an oath. "Could we talk about something else? You understand."

Davis was certain he understood. To prevent the alternative question about how his Compressor Carrier worked, he quickly excused himself, sliding past Timmerman, who drew his feet underneath his seat but left his big knees protruding like howitzers.

With the rest room's small door locked behind him, Davis stood with closed eyes, feeling the rolling terrain of air passing underneath his feet. Here, more than anywhere else on the plane, he knew he was flying, the thrust and rush throbbing in his hips and spine; in his arms and legs, the loose-jointedness of a thrown marionette. Shoulder against the outside wall, he let the cold seep in, the icy brittleness of the thin atmosphere, and pulled out his insulin syringe. He studied it the way he had seen junkies do in television exposés of drug abuse. The magic needle, himself just one more wreck in need of a fix.

Having to guess how much, he squeezed a thread into the sink, then held the needle above a pinch of flesh and waited for the moment. Strange to hesitate after more than a dozen years. Stranger still to feel the magic of the instant when it could be done, when the mind turned to stone and the eyes looked without seeing. Now—and it was over.

A woman waiting outside the door gave an impatient sigh when Davis bumbled past her. Something in the tight line of her lips suggested disgust. Davis was about to say "It's only heroin" when the door clicked shut. Stupid to think she could know what he had done. He unconsciously patted his shirt pocket to be sure he hadn't left the syringe behind. So what if she did know? What if everyone knew? Looking down the long row alive at the edges with arms and legs, he thought of insects, a burrow pocketed with lives. Maybe they sensed his disease in the telepathic way insects know the wounded and the near-dead among them. Grasping each seat back for balance, he felt himself moving along a swinging bridge. Below was the abyss. Uninterpretable.

When the snack came, a doll-sized sandwich with a pretend bag of chips puffed up by altitude, Davis asked for orange juice. Timmerman reached for it and seemed about to take a sip before he handed it over, saying, "Here you go." Then, as he unwrapped his sandwich, he asked Davis, "How many people do you think would fit in here if all the air were squeezed out of them?"

"You'd do better to squeeze the water out of 'em."

Timmerman grunted approval, then lapsed into what must have been a serious consideration of the options. The process kept him quiet as he compressed one way and then another, loading his flattened or dehydrated people onto Timmerman's One-way Airline.

To have made it this far, midway between Des Moines and Nashville, without revealing a single personal detail, liberated Davis. He could be anyone on his way anywhere, his real identity as an academic second-stringer a secret, hidden partially even from himself. Entering the white noise of windsweep and turbines, he fell asleep thinking of Ben Blau and his doomed invention, of Timmerman's creation of doom; and in his dream he opened a satchel filled with compacted lives, each in a thin folder, strange pressed leaves. He saw himself filing his mother, the label "Ellen Banks" protruding until he tamped the edges flush with all the rest, and she was gone.

•

Some dreams are awakened from, others into. As Davis opened his eyes, blinking away the vision of finished and filed lives, he held very still to give his mind a chance to level itself. He was on a plane, en route to Tennessee to arrange the details of his mother's funeral. The call had come that morning, while he was at work. Not entirely unexpected, because of her bad heart. Why, then, did he still feel he was dreaming? Turning to his left, he saw Timmerman rising and falling in his seat like a weightless astronaut as the plane bounded moguls of air. Yes, his mother was dead, even if he was Ben Blau and not Davis Banks. A parentless son by any other name. . . . Too frivolous to finish.

Fully awake now, he took inventory: forty-five and orphaned by death. Father gone for eight years. No brothers or sisters. One more file waiting—his own.

He felt a sudden urge to tell Timmerman the truth, but the dry air snapped with the pilot's voice announcing their descent into Nashville. Nothing to do now but hold on in silence. No difference, anyway. Timmerman wouldn't know what to say and might resent the original lie, or he might not know which version to believe and become patronizing. Medal of Honor winner. Timmerman didn't deserve the truth, didn't really even deserve a story as good as the one Davis had told him.

Dragging his shoulder bag over the seats, he pushed into line behind Timmerman, realizing for the first time how tall the man was. At least six feet four, several inches taller than Davis, taller than anyone else on the plane. Maybe he truly was a war hero. Vietnam. The war Davis missed because the lottery tagged him number 301. He didn't exactly regret being lucky, but sometimes he wished he could truthfully say to someone like Timmerman, "Hey, man, I was in-country, too." Assuming, of course, that Timmerman was there. Davis closed his eyes and thought of the two of them in the jungle, faces streaked with camouflage. What would Timmerman do to win the medal? What would Davis Banks do to keep from dying?

Someone nudged Davis from behind and said, "Line's moving," making him realize that Timmerman and everyone ahead of him had gone. Not Vietnam. Nashville. How could he have flashbacks of a war he was never in—belly-down in mud, the rain a waterfall on his back? A voice in his head said, "Post-traumatic number 301 syndrome."

When he walked into one of the waiting areas just beyond the ramp door, he was sweating, and other passengers were staring at him. He looked down at himself as though splattered with blood and then said, to no one in particular, "My mother

just died." At first, his lips formed the words but no sound
came. Then more breath than sound, "My mother just died,"
followed by an aimless turning until a flight attendant took him
by the arm and helped him sit down. "Sugar," he said blankly.
Her head tilted toward him as if she were waiting for a kiss.
Then the whole building tipped, and he heard somewhere in
his brain a sustained car horn in a mall parking lot, and he
knew it was too late to find it and stop it. The blare soaked and
pulled him under.

·

"You've gotta give him a few more minutes." A southern voice
in the blankness. "Here, take another bite." He realized, then,
he was chewing. "When I saw that little pouch sticking out of
his shoulder bag, I knew what was wrong. Diabetic kit, just like
my daddy's." The gray kit now lay open, exposing syringes, a
blood monitor, blood-test strips, and a single vial of insulin.
"Nothing to worry about as long as he comes around." As the
room re-created itself, a young man blurred over Davis. "Can
you hear me?" Davis thought he nodded, but the question
came again and he tried to say yes. When he saw the half-eaten
candy bar in the young man's hand, Davis grabbed it and took
the rest into his mouth in a single bite. "He'll be fine," the voice
said. "Exactly like my daddy."

"Seen one diabetic, you've seen 'em all," Davis said through
the chocolate and caramel, his belligerence returning first.

"Hell, you must have known my daddy," the young man
said with a laugh. "He had a smart mouth, too, when the insulin zapped him."

Davis gave him what he thought was a withering look, but
it produced only a laugh. "He's out of danger now." Then the
man was gone, though a small group stalled nearby. The flight
attendant asked if she should get a doctor, and Davis said, "No.

No, I'll be all right." When she asked again, Davis leaned toward her, and spoke with emphasis, as if she didn't entirely understand English, *"No doctor."* She stood and clipped her way down the concourse, leaving him slumped in his chair.

As the world returned, Davis began the critical self-assessment that always followed such episodes. Too much insulin. A low blood sugar before the injection so that the stingy airline snack wasn't enough. And he needed to be more careful with the fast-acting Humalog. Now he wanted to thank the man who gave him the candy and apologize to the flight attendant who stayed with him. Too complicated to explain that when the sugar is gone, the brain turns bitter in its brine.

Moving to the rest room, Davis felt his strength returning, but he worried about those moments he couldn't remember, when he had eaten half a candy bar and been surrounded by gawkers. Did he grunt as he ate? Where was his mind while his body was hunched in primordial hunger? In the mirror, he saw his chin streaked with chocolate, the corners of his mouth stained brown. The face was his, but it had been somewhere else, attached to someone he didn't know. Ben Blau. Treacherous son of a bitch, running off with his face. And where was Timmerman when a hero was needed? Big Medal of Honor Winner should have been there shouting, "Medic! Medic!" Why hadn't he leaned over him, whispering, "You're gonna make it, buddy"?

"Shit." Until the man at the next sink looked up, Davis didn't know he had said the word aloud. Trying a faint grin, he turned back to the mirror and rubbed at the chocolate. Even cleaned up, he looked like a man who had fallen from a window and been saved by the limber branches of a tree. Tucking in his damp shirttail, he watched himself become Davis Banks once more, the color returning, some light in his eyes, a boyishness behind his glum mask. Forcing a smile, he persuaded himself he could be mistaken for someone in his mid-thirties, a big, athletic type. Maybe he should invent a running shoe or some sports equipment. The Verticalizer. Guaranteed to improve posture and increase height by properly aligning the vertebrae. But what would it be? Something lightweight, easily worn under clothing. Yes, he could sell it.

Davis stretched to his full height, turned sideways, and tensed his stomach. Now he was himself, or maybe Arch Steel, inventor of the Verticalizer. Still jittery from insulin shock, he couldn't hold the pose. He was Davis Banks, and a suitcase riding the baggage carousel would be tagged with that name.

CHAPTER 2

DAVIS WOULD HAVE preferred to rent a car for the forty-mile
drive north to Clarksville, but he knew someone would be at
the airport to meet him, probably one of his younger cousins
with a modified Chevy, jacked up in the rear by huge racing
slicks, Nirvana and Alabama on the tape player. Loud speed
and no chance for conversation, a screaming privacy. Instead,
he found Uncle Oscar studying the conveyor, the unclaimed
bags moving only a little slower than the old man drove. Wearing his usual combination of suspenders and a belt, he was the
perfect emblem of caution. When he saw Davis approaching,
he waved broadly enough to be guiding a jet to the ramp and
started talking even before his voice was audible.

"Awful, just awful," he was saying as Davis sloughed his shoulder bag and clenched his arms across his chest. "A shock, I know, but the Good Lord has his reasons; yessir, the Good Lord knows what we don't."

Resisting an impulse to strike the old man, Davis tightened his arms and took a step back. "How'd you get stuck with this taxi service?"

"Volunteered, I reckon. Everybody else was wore out or just too down, 'specially your aunt Goldie. Your mama's only sister, you know, and she's grievin' hard. Anyway, I wanted to talk. Ain't seen you in forever."

The worst was going to happen. Oscar, the Baptist lay minister, was going to witness. Sanctimonious Oscar, the man with all the answers, because one answer served for every question: "The Good Lord has his ways." When Oscar intoned, "We never know when our name will be called. Could be anybody at any time," his arm sweeping the entire baggage area, Davis wished it had been Oscar instead of his mother. What possible plan of God's would rank Oscar over Ellen Banks? Like privileging a weed above an iris. Davis wanted him yanked out and a cup of salt poured in the hole with the roots.

Beyond Uncle Oscar's prophetic arm, Davis glimpsed his bag about to disappear through the plastic strips at the far end of the conveyor, and bolted to grab it, skating the last few feet on the slick tile, feeling almost giddy.

"It would've been back, son; no need to break your neck. What goes around comes around."

By the time they found the car in the parking garage and drove through the toll gate, Oscar had expanded considerably upon his don't-ask-because-God's-not-telling theology. Davis imagined a bumper sticker for Oscar's puttering car: HE'S GOD, THAT'S WHY. Might be a useful idea for the flight back to Des Moines—the inventor of stickers for all beliefs, including nonbelief—WAVE IF YOU'RE JESUS. Who would be the first to signal? And what would happen then?

Davis had never known how Oscar got the call. Whether he actually heard a voice or simply had a feeling wasn't clear, probably not even to Oscar, who always said, "I just knew what the Good Lord wanted me to do and I done it." Could have been indigestion or maybe a small cerebral hemorrhage. God's tuning in to Oscar's frequency and giving him a life mission was too scary to contemplate.

"Your mama was a good woman, son, a good woman; and she's in heaven right now, with Jesus. Because everything was right between her and the Good Lord. Oh, I know she was quick-tempered and said things sometimes, but in her heart she was good. She done the best she could."

Davis marveled that "preachy old windbag" wasn't audible, his thoughts telepathically penetrating Oscar's denseness. Davis concentrated: *Oscar, if you hear me, honk the horn. This is God. Honk if you hear me.* Oscar clicked the headlights on to high beam. "Almost," Davis mused, as the car passed the fringe lighting of the city and headed into darkness.

Davis tracked the headlights as they raced the pavement, the car winding out of Nashville and climbing the west side of the Cumberland Basin. He remembered making this trip with his parents on the old highway, stopping once for hamburgers at a malt stand in Germantown on the very top of the hill. Now there wasn't even a sign on the interstate for the little settlement, everything bypassed and left to clog from disuse.

"Can we get something to eat? I didn't have much on the plane."

"Lordy, son, there's enough food at home to feed everyone in Montgomery County. Can't you hold out for another half hour?"

How could he explain to one-answer Oscar that when the

diabetic's brain says eat it means *now*. Probably what had happened in the airport was making him overcautious. Maybe his blood sugar level was off the high end of the scale, as sometimes happened when he mistook highs for lows. Still, he was hungry. His head fell back against the seat as his father's death returned in a vision of potato salad, fried chicken, pot roasts, three-bean salad, corn bread, ham, turnip greens, and every kind of pie imaginable. The house foundered with food, and everyone who stopped by to pay respects was fed, people sitting with paper plates on their knees, the food giving them something to talk about, or filling their mouths so they didn't have to speak of death.

As Davis's ears popped with the incline, he knew Germantown was somewhere off to the left, blocked out by trees and limestone bluffs, its little burger stand in ruins on a highway no one used anymore. Uncle Oscar's voice, droning about the sweet bosom of our Lord, and the car's engine melded, holding a soporific pitch that matched the tired humming in Davis's bones, making him want to close his eyes and sleep. He always rested well whenever he came here, and it nettled him to think he might have been meant to stay in Tennessee, where something soothing invited him to lie down. Or was it sinister, serpentine, the old entanglements of southern blood?

"Have some of my french fries," his mother said from the backseat, handing the paper sleeve over Davis's shoulder. "I can't eat 'em all, and I'm sure you're hungry after your trip. Hard to beat the fries at that little place in Germantown."

"You say something?" asked Uncle Oscar. "I thought you were asleep."

"Uh, no, nothing," said Davis, clearing his throat. "Sorry. Just dozed off for a minute, I guess."

"More like twenty, I'd say. We're nearly to the Clarksville exit."

Even in the dark, the landscape was familiar: rolling hills covered with scrubby cedars, here and there a limestone outcropping or red-clay gully. Davis felt the old connection and detachment coming on: like the flash of intimacies upon meeting a former lover, the awkward amenities and the sure knowledge that nothing could ever be as it was. But how was it, exactly, beyond the myth and wishfulness? What blood ritual made him forever southern? Even as a boy, he thought of himself as southern, a mark of pride, a fine old family name—one of the Southerners.

"How's it feel to be home?" Uncle Oscar intruded, as though still receiving messages from Davis's mind.

"Home?" The word was pure exhalation, a blow to the diaphragm, the kind of word that could be final, the last breath of the dying. Clarksville had sprawled in the last nine years, and streets with unfamiliar names flashed by the window. To Davis, it was still a little river town with a Piggly Wiggly grocery and Ben Franklin five-and-dime, still the place where soldiers from Fort Campbell's 101st Airborne division came across the Kentucky state line to get drunk and scuffle with the local boys over women. Home.

"I'll run you by our place for something to eat and then carry you on over to your mama's," Oscar offered.

"No, no, that's all right. I'm not hungry anymore," he lied. "Besides, I'm sure I can find something to snack on at home." There was that word again, sudden as a twitch.

"There won't be much, son. You know how your mama was about food."

"No," Davis said, baiting his uncle, "how was she?"

"Let's just say she was a picky eater." Oscar's deft sidestepping surprised Davis, and they fell silent until the intersection of the street where Oscar and Aunt Goldie lived. "Sure you won't change your mind? We've got pecan pie so good it'll make your tongue knock your eyeteeth out." Davis's grunt and nod could have been interpreted either way, but Oscar read them as rejection and drove on without protest.

As the car crept away from the curb, Davis stood in his mother's front yard, knowing the old man didn't really want him at his house. Strange to be dumped. Should be on the other end of the process, Oscar standing in a dark ditch outside of town, fighting his rage with false forgiveness as Davis screeched away.

The night air made him feel better—early April, a richness in the breeze, the scent of everything stirring. Across the street, a dogwood tree in full bloom generated its own light, soft and cold, like the moon's. Walking around the house, looking at the windows and the dark roofline, Davis laughed when he saw his mother's old car hulking in the driveway. He sauntered around it, smiling when he thought of his nickname for it, the Trackless Tank. But even derision couldn't persuade her to get a smaller car, something she could parallel park. "If I'm in a wreck, I don't want them to have to pry me loose from the metal," she would say. "Give me a big car with plenty of hood out in front."

Imagining he was a car thief, Davis quietly tried the doors and wondered if locking them had been one of his mother's last acts. His throat tightened, and he kicked one of the tires so hard a kind of voltage ran up his leg and his toes went numb.

Through the windows he saw a plastic rain scarf on the front seat—"my shower cap," she used to say—and a paperback book, lying facedown. Probably titled *Tempestuous Love* or *Passionate Affair.* His mother inhaled cheap romances, reading them even at stoplights, the cars behind beeping when the red went green.

Continuing around the house, Davis was startled by something at the far end of the backyard. It looked like someone bent over to tie a shoe. As he drew near, it became a lawn mower. Stopped exactly at the end of a single mown strip, it waited for someone to turn it around and finish the job. He poked the almost empty bag with his tingling foot.

When the back light came on at the house next door, Davis stepped into the shadows. He could see a face in the kitchen window, the neighbor sighting down the spotlight beam that ignited her weedy lawn. His mother had probably checked out noises the same way, and this was how she looked to the burglar, the voyeur, the murderer. When the light went out, Davis knew the face was still there, even though he couldn't see it. She was waiting for him to move, but her mind would quickly reason him away. He was only her imagination or the wind. Stiffening himself in the darkness, he felt invisible, dangerous.

The front door swung open to the unmistakable smell of ammonia, and Davis stopped just inside. His mother had never been much of a housekeeper, so it was hard to imagine her scouring the oven or scrubbing some corner of her yellowed kitchen floor. With the streetlight's illumination through the open door, Davis could make out newspapers scattered on the sofa and an afghan piled on the floor, as if his mother had just stood up to greet him, letting it slide off her lap.

When he turned on the light, the room he knew by heart materialized, with its salmon-colored carpet and matching end-table lamps made of old porcelain jugs, the coffee table piled with magazines. At the far end, a wall covered with photographs outlined in a flash of moments the story of his life through all its gawky, awkward stages, right up until he left for Des Moines nine years ago.

A small motor whined somewhere behind him—the VCR recording. When he turned on the set, the screen slowly filled with the watercolor look of a fifties movie, thin pigments a good rain might wash off, returning everything to black and white, a man and a woman arguing in a sports car. Davis muted the sound and watched them drive along, their mouths moving in what could have been song; then he hummed a mock finale and, with an operatic flourish, killed the picture.

In the refrigerator, he found a package of American cheese and a mayonnaise jar filled with tea—"Made by Mama," he thought, holding up the garnet liquid to study it in the overhead light. A search of the kitchen cabinets turned up plain crackers, so he peeled the cellophane wrapping off four slices of cheese, broke each one into quadrants, and made a small stack of the squares, alternating them with crackers, just as he had done as a child.

"Playing with your food again," his mother would say, in a tone halfway between question and allegation. "At least get a plate to put things on."

Davis balanced his tower on a saucer and went back into the living room. The most recent newspaper was two days old. He knew his mother would have bought it at the Quick Shop on her way home from work. "No sense in paying extra to have it delivered," she'd say.

The headline was vintage Clarksville: MAYOR FILES PEACE BOND AGAINST POLITICAL FOE. Underneath, exactly in the middle of the page, was a photo of a mangled car with the caption "Two killed in early morning accident. Story page 3." Davis leafed through to read the unfamiliar names.

Had he stayed in Clarksville, would he grieve for these people? Would he take sides in the mayor's fight with the opponent who had threatened to "reach down his lyin' throat and jerk him inside out"?

Davis swallowed a square of cheese and shook his head, remembering when he finally gave up trying to live in the same town with his parents and relatives. Having his own duplex apartment here hadn't been the same as having his own life, because someone, usually his mother, was always dialing his number or standing on the front steps ringing the bell. Looking back, he realized he had been little more than a kid on an extended outing, especially after his marriage failed. He had let Linda have all the furniture and then camped out inside the shell of their former home.

When the phone crashed his thoughts, Davis stood up so quickly he banged his shin on the coffee table and sent the empty saucer wobbling on edge across the room like a lost wheel.

Trying to recover his breath, he stood next to the phone in the hallway and rubbed his throbbing leg, finally answering to a voice that said, "Praise the Good Lord, you're all right." It was Aunt Goldie, who normally would have been in bed three hours earlier. She had obviously stayed up to monitor Davis's activities while deciding which jewelry to wear with her black funeral dress.

"You been running, Davis? You sound plumb out of breath."

"No, no, I'm all right. Just sitting here reading the paper and thinking about going to bed."

"I called you four or five times after Oscar got back. Why didn't you answer?"

"I was on the back steps, looking at the stars and getting a little air. Airplanes are so stuffy." He lied to avoid the burden of explaining why he'd stalled so long before coming inside. Anyhow, he wasn't sure he could make sense of it. "Why are you still up?"

"Worried sick about you, child. You should have stopped here for something to eat. You'd have slept better."

"No chance of not sleeping tonight," he said, faking a loud yawn. "See what I mean?"

"Well, get in the bed and rest up for tomorrow. We'll see you over here in the morning for biscuits and gravy. All right?"

Davis held the line, but when Goldie queried a second time, he had no choice but to answer yes.

His mother's bed was the only one in the house, since Davis's had been removed years ago and his old room turned into a large storage closet. At Christmas and on other occasions, he slept compacted on the sofa. Now there was no reason not to be more comfortable. When he opened the bedroom door, he saw the bed was unmade, left just the way his mother had rolled out of it the last time.

In the bathroom, he located the source of the ammonia smell, an opened bottle of drain cleaner beside the toilet. He poured the contents into the bowl and flushed.

After brushing his teeth, he checked the doors. "Still the same old worrier, aren't you?" He could imagine his mother standing behind him in pajamas and bathrobe. "Even when you were a little boy you traipsed through the house every night, making sure the screens were latched and all the doors locked tight."

It was true. He was compulsive—about securing the doors, especially—believing the responsibility fell solely on him. No one else knew how to test the locks by turning the doorknobs the correct number of times and tugging with the right amount of force. Sometimes, after everyone had gone to bed, he would slip through the house to check the doors again, unable to sleep until the ritual had been performed in a way that felt completely satisfying.

From his diabetic kit, Davis took a tube of glucose tablets and his blood sugar monitor and placed them on the night table. Although he normally slept in only a T-shirt and underwear, he put on his pajamas, as he always did when visiting his mother, and slid beneath the covers before he could act on the impulse to take them off.

The sheets were pilly, and the pillowcase smelled of hair

spray. As he shifted from one side to the other, tipping on the brink of sleep, something beneath the covers touched his back. For a moment he held still, trying to decide if he was dreaming; but the blood roaring through his head convinced him he was awake. At the small of his back, just above his hips, something pressed lightly.

Davis swung the covers off and cartwheeled out of bed, slapping the wall to find the light switch near the doorway. Trying to slow his heart and breath, he turned and saw a pillow, placed halfway down one side of the bed. In an instant, he understood its purpose—something to fill the space, not a surrogate bedmate but something tactile under the covers, a point of reference other than the self when the light went out.

After his father's death, Davis's mother had insisted she was all right alone; over the years, she had never seemed afraid. But now he felt neglectful and selfish. He stood for a long time, seeing his mother pressed up against her secret companion or stretching an arm across it in her sleep.

Tugging the blankets off the bed, he dragged them into the living room and spread them on the sofa. Knowing it was late, he turned to look at the clock, but he couldn't see it in the dark, couldn't see anything as he remembered how his mother always called from her room, "Good night, darlin'; sleep tight."

CHAPTER 3

BUCK OWENS WAS singing "... and all I gotta do is act naturally" when Davis untangled himself from sleep and remembered he was in his mother's house. "She'll be fixing breakfast," he thought. But as he swung around to sit up on the sofa, the emptiness embraced him, the cold envelopment of the original news. This time, though, he wasn't taking it well, wasn't as stoic and composed as when the call came just one day ago. After that, time had somehow lagged, enlisting him to drag its load of seconds, minutes, hours up a sharp incline. Yesterday should be a blur in the valley but was, instead, a near-miss boulder tumbled onto the path immediately behind him.

"It's six-twenty in Clarksville, Gateway to the New South,

on a beautiful spring day, so jump outta that bed and get to it," a voice said, and then a commercial for Hughes Used Cars screeched out of control.

He followed the breathless voice to the nightstand beside his mother's bed. A clock radio shone a sickly orange, the disc jockey pattering about tax deadlines and the IRS hiding in the bushes. When Davis pressed the alarm button, 6:00 A.M. flashed across the display. "When she always got up," he thought, "and when she would have been up today." He tapped the off button, then leaned over to straighten the sheet, pulling it over the companion pillow, which bulged like someone small and very tired.

Shaved, showered, and on his way to the living room and his suitcase, Davis leaned into the bedroom to see the time. As his eyes scanned past the numbers glowing 7:30, he saw that the sheet was rumpled and the pillow exposed. Frozen in place, clutching the knot of the towel wrapped around him at the waist, he remembered stretching across the bed to make the corners even and and was almost certain he had looked back before leaving the room. Maybe he hadn't done such a neat job. Then again. . . . "Don't play games, Mama. I'm not in the mood." He emphasized every word as though performing an exorcism. Nothing answered.

In the living room, as Davis bent over his suitcase to rummage for socks, his head filled with a freeway rush and he could hear his own labored breathing from a great distance. "Eat something," a faraway voice insisted. In the dining room, a pair of spotted bananas he had missed last night lay in their wooden bowl, sodden with ripeness. He swallowed each in two sour bites, then gulped a glass of water and sat down to wait for the sugar rush while performing his litany of recriminations: "Should check blood sugars more often, should eat on a regular schedule, shouldn't play games with eyes, kidneys, life. Could end up whittled down to a wheelchair."

His mother had used overripe bananas for banana pudding, mashing the bruised crescents into a sucking pulp, adding plenty of sugar to cover the decay, layering little wafers and burying everything in meringue. The light on the carpet was the color of pudding gone bad, and Davis felt the bananas rising in his throat. "Calm, calm. Deep breaths." He waited. The whole house smelled of bananas, his mother's concoction cooling.

As Davis recovered, he felt his anger rising, as it often did after insulin reactions. "Damned disease! Thoughtful gift from my mother." Then he argued against his own bitterness, "Unfair. Not her fault."

And yet diabetes lurked on her side of the family, skipping generations, missing her and finding him. Pointless to go through this rage, but he hated himself for the flaw, the failure that defined him. Hated her for the inheritance. Hated himself again for hating her. It was a closed loop within which he circled himself. "Stop," he commanded, thrusting out of orbit.

Knowing he needed more food, he looked for the keys to his mother's car. She usually left them hanging from the ring with the door key in the lock, but they weren't there. When a cursory search failed to turn them up elsewhere, Davis suddenly realized he didn't know where his mother had died. He assumed the end had come at home; yet if she died at someone else's house, whoever brought the car back could have kept the keys.

When Aunt Goldie had phoned him at work in Des Moines, she had said only, "I've got awful bad news for you, darlin'," never uttering the word "dead" because everything could be extrapolated from her broad, dark announcement and somber tone. Within minutes, Davis had made airline reservations and was on his way home to pack, never considering the logistics of his mother's death.

Death's mechanics now became supremely important. He had assumed her heart gave out from the years of chronic angina, yet no one actually had told him that. During the car trip from the airport, Uncle Oscar had described the whereabouts of each family member when news of Ellen's death came, had given those details with the precision of pins in a map; but he hadn't mentioned where the death had occurred, or its cause.

The need to know everything began to overshadow Davis's grief, and the dullness and anger following his low blood sugar were overwhelmed by anxiety. "Gotta think this through. Where's her purse?"

He was up again, moving frantically through the house. No purse anywhere. "Damn! Have to be logical about this. If she had an attack here and called for an ambulance, she could have taken it with her to the hospital." But anyone experiencing the pain of a heart attack wouldn't give a shit about her purse; she'd just want help.

Davis was dialing Oscar's number when it occurred to him there was probably a spare set of keys somewhere, a thought that brought relief, as nothing could be worse than being chauffeured by Oscar. And if he made the call, Goldie would tighten the noose of her breakfast invitation.

Now the search changed from obvious places to cabinets and closets. "Out of sight but handy," he reasoned as he yanked out bureau drawers. When he lifted the small vase on his mother's dresser, something metallic chattered inside, and he dumped the contents into his palm—a small ring of keys, two for the Ford, one for the house, and a fourth that Davis didn't recognize. "All right!" he exulted. "Something's finally going right."

As he put the vase down, he saw himself in the mirror, unknown for a split second: a middle-aged man with a youngish look, tall and sallow-faced, a slight crease at the corners of his mouth. "God, I look awful," he said aloud, touching a forefinger to the puffy spot under one of his eyes. Then, backing up, he stood in profile. "Not bad for forty-five," he rationalized, lost in time. When his focus shifted and he could see the bed reflected behind him, the companion pillow peeking from under the sheet, he felt foolish, as if he'd been discovered in his vanity. "You idiot," he said, leaning forward, almost touching his nose to the face looking back.

Shaking the keys as if they were dice, Davis stepped out the back door into a balmy morning. He had forgotten how mild the early spring days were in Tennessee. Nothing like Iowa, where no one dared put even a potted fern on the porch before mid-May, when the last freeze date was past.

Before starting the car, he picked up the paperback lying on the passenger seat and shook his head at the title: *Rebellion of the Passionate Heart*. "I guessed almost right," he thought, flipping the pages until he came to a turned-down corner halfway through:

Tiffany had always been willful, even headstrong, and she was accustomed to having her own way. But there was something about Brock's indifference that excited her, made her want to yield.

Davis closed the book and tossed it onto the backseat, laughing in short exhalations through his nose at the thought of his mother eagerly turning the pages to watch poor little Tiffany gradually brought under the control of dominating Brock.

His mother was anything but submissive, had been the dominant force in her own marriage, holding down a job and running the household. "I've got better things to do with my time than dust bric-a-brac," she used to pronounce. And Davis remembered how unyielding she was in any argument.

The old car sputtered, so Davis let it idle for a minute; when he accelerated to pull out of the driveway, the noise evened into a full roar. "What a jalopy," he thought, imagining all the neighbors peeking out their windows as he rumbled down the street.

It was nearly nine o'clock, and the breakfast rush was over at Red's Bakery on Riverside Drive. Without checking his blood sugar, Davis ordered a cream horn and a glazed cinnamon bun. Better to err on the side of blood sugar highs today than to risk another insulin reaction. Anyhow, he had left his blood monitor and insulin in the car. Tucking his Medic Alert bracelet underneath his shirt cuff, he pretended to himself that he was normal and could eat whatever he wanted.

The morning paper was lying on a table in the corner, and as Davis flipped through it, sipping coffee, the obituaries caught his eye. In an inky box was a picture of his mother, one he hadn't seen before, younger and prettier than Davis remembered. Beneath the photo were the standard details for the dead:

Mrs. Ellen Banks, 64, wife of Mr. Ralph Banks, deceased, died early Wednesday morning. She is survived by a son, Davis, presently of Des Moines. Services will be held at 2 P.M. Saturday, at Berkley's Funeral Home.

The starkness of the black-and-white picture and the directness of the little blurb made Davis breathless, as if he'd been pushed from behind and was falling down a great chasm. Standing up abruptly, he tipped over his coffee. "Shit!" he muttered, oblivious to the other people in the room. "Goddamn it!"

A waitress rushed over with a damp towel and mopped at the spill. "Don't worry, sugar, I'll get you another cup," she said, giving Davis a sidelong look as he stood motionless, arms drawn back, fingers spread as if disavowing responsibility.

When he saw that everyone was staring at him, he muttered "Sorry. Got the night-shift spasms" to no one in particular, then careened for the door, rubbing his eyes and faking a big yawn. When he got to the car, he realized he still had the newspaper. Folding the pages to his mother's smiling face, he propped the paper on the steering wheel.

"Died early Wednesday. What the hell does that mean?" Of course *The Clarksville Leaf Chronicle* never provided the cause of anyone's death, out of a longtime tradition of deference to the families. Readers were left awash in speculation and rumors often much worse than the true story. Ellen Banks could have hanged herself with an extension cord, for all anyone knew. For all Davis knew.

•

When he arrived at Berkley's Funeral Home, the door was locked, but someone heard him jiggling the handle and came at once.

"Sorry, forgot to open up at nine. I've been so busy since I got here early this morning that it just slipped my mind. I'm Mr. Berkley."

Davis shook the extended hand, which held his a few seconds longer than he expected.

"And you are . . . ?" asked Mr. Berkley, his voice rising with the last word.

"Banks. Davis Banks." He felt odd admitting his true identity so readily.

"Ah, yes, Mr. Banks. It's your mother, isn't it?" Mr. Berkley asked rhetorically, tipping his bald head down to look over the top of his glasses.

This was going to be worse than Davis had imagined. He had always hated funerals, and this unctuous little man seemed to guarantee that this one would be particularly loathsome.

"Well, please come to my office. Would you like some coffee?"

"No thanks," Davis replied, fixing his gaze on the fleur-de-lis pattern in the carpet as he walked.

The office was upstairs, at the end of a labyrinth of hallways. Luther Berkley had taken over this rambling antebellum house twenty years ago and completely remodeled the inside to suit his death business, making the elegant mansion a perfect emblem of the New South. From the street, the brick facade and white columns evoked images of an earlier time; but inside, the place was a maze of gloomy rooms with sliding partitions and doors that folded back against the walls.

Settling into a leather swivel chair behind a large mahogany desk, Mr. Berkley said, "I'm so sorry about your mother."

"Did you know her?"

"Well, yes, of course. We met eight years ago when your father died."

"How did she end up here?"

"I don't think you understand, Mr. Banks. Your mother made all the arrangements eight years ago—for her own burial. When she took care of your father's affairs, she also made arrangements for herself."

"What kind of 'arrangements'?" Davis asked, sarcastically emphasizing Mr. Berkley's vague word.

"Why, all of them, of course. Our pre-need plan takes care of everything—mortician fees, coffin, burial—everything." As he said this, Mr. Berkley rolled closer to his desk and spread his hands across the blotter in a proprietary way.

"You mean my mother paid you in advance for her own funeral?" Davis sounded incredulous even to himself. He wondered where she got the money before realizing it had come from his father's life insurance.

"That's right. Eight years ago."

"She never mentioned it to me."

"That's not so unusual. People don't want to upset the family. You don't have to do a thing, Mr. Banks. Not one little thing. As I said, our pre-need plan takes care of everything. It's a pity we had to discontinue the program a few years ago. Costs, you know. But we're standing behind all our earlier contracts, naturally. Would you care to view the body?"

There was a business-as-usual flatness to this invitation, but the words "view the body" startled Davis. He knew he wasn't ready for that and flashed to the time he had last seen his mother. It was Christmas, when they had gotten on each other's nerves.

"I don't care what you do," she had said, emphasizing the word "what" as if it were something unspeakable. "You're hardly here long enough to call it a visit, anyway, so just go on back to Des Moines."

As always, they patched it up and parted on decent terms; but his last memory of her was that evening when she tried to wheedle him into staying past the twenty-sixth. Her strategy in all arguments was to disguise her last offensive as total surrender, and Davis could still see her fanning out the newspaper to erect a partition between them, pretending to read but really waiting for him to acquiesce.

"You all right, Mr. Banks? Mr. Banks?"

"Yes . . . yes, I'm fine," said Davis, half gone into the rest of his reverie—an unsettling vision of his mother laid out, somewhere in a dead-end corner of the maze. "Just fine."

"Well . . . would you like to view the body?" offered Mr. Berkley a second time.

"Yes, I suppose." His answer surprised him, because he definitely did not want to see his mother's corpse. A sense of duty had overruled his fear, the way a parent takes a child by the hand and leads him into the antiseptic smell of the doctor's examination room.

Mr. Berkley asked him to wait in the hallway while he went into the room—"to turn on the lights," he said—but he was gone longer than the time it would take to flip a switch. When he finally returned, he said, "Now we can step in."

The small room was filled with about forty folding chairs, set up to leave a broad aisle down the middle. Directly opposite the door, the coffin stood in front of a wall of burgundy curtains. The lid at one end was propped open, but from where he stood Davis couldn't see anything; and as he shuffled forward, he kept his eyes on the curtains, letting his mother's face come slowly into the periphery of vision.

She looked natural. It was a cliché, what everyone said at funerals, whether they meant it or not; but Ellen Banks looked natural. "Oh, Mama!" he said, just above a whisper. He had expected her to look waxen, artificial, like a bad replica of herself, so the shock of seeing his mother exactly as he remembered her sent a tremor through his legs. Backing up, eyes fixed on that familiar profile, he sat down on one of the folding chairs.

Finally, he had the fact of her death firsthand, not long-distance over the telephone or in an empty house his mother might reenter at any moment, but in the still, unmistakable form holding its breath before him. "Outside of time," he thought, and then felt silly for the euphemism. "Dead," he said aloud. "My mother is dead." He turned to speak to Mr. Berkley, but discovered he had discreetly withdrawn.

Davis approached the coffin again, this time studying his mother's dress—a blue one he didn't remember—and the way her hands were folded so her wedding ring was visible. The coffin was stained a dark walnut, with brass handles and a white satin lining. Davis looked behind the heavy curtains, curious to know if they covered a window, but found only a wall.

Leaving the room quickly, he surprised Mr. Berkley loitering in the hallway, trying to conceal a cigarette.

"Filthy habit," he said, extinguishing the coals on the sole of his shoe. "Ought to quit."

"You're sure you don't need anything from me?" Davis asked. "I mean, don't we need to schedule things?"

"All the details have been taken care of by your relatives, Mr. Banks. You just put your mind at ease."

Outside, Davis paused on the steps and breathed deeply. Directly ahead at the end of the parking lot, two redbuds were in full color. "Spring," he said to himself, sounding the word as if he had just uncovered a hoax. He pulled off his sweater and pitched it onto the backseat before getting into the car; when he had started the engine, he sat, thinking of nothing in particular, lost in the deep rumble of the exhaust.

Responding to several short taps on the window, he turned full into the simpering face of Mr. Berkley, whose cheek almost touched the glass.

"Glad I caught you," he said, trying to make himself heard over the roar. Davis killed the engine and rolled the window down halfway. "There *is* something I need from you. We'll have a limousine for the immediate family. You know, to follow right behind the hearse. But we can only handle six people. It'll save a lot of confusion if you can pick the six before the ceremony. Nothing's worse than having everybody wandering around the parking lot after the service while we try to get all the cars lined up for the procession."

Saying nothing, Davis turned the key in the ignition and pressed hard on the gas. The engine started in a great, stammering eruption, causing Mr. Berkley to jump back. As he pulled out of the lot, Davis glanced in the mirror to see him standing with his hands hanging loosely at his sides.

CHAPTER 4

UNACCUSTOMED TO SUCH a lumbering car, Davis ran the rear wheels over the curb when he turned onto Madison Street and headed downtown. Deadtown. Not much reason to go there anymore, except to conduct business at the courthouse. Gone the days of parakeets at Woolworth's, toys at the back of McClellan's, the pricey dresses at Mademoiselle's. One of the two old theaters had endured, the Roxy, used now for amateur productions of *Bye Bye Birdie* and *Waiting for Godot.*

As he turned onto Franklin Street, an oncoming car sounded its horn and the driver screamed something while pointing up at the one-way sign. Davis pounded the wheel and held his hands palm up, yelling, "I didn't know they'd changed the goddamned street!" But the other driver didn't hear, his face red, fist pressed into the steering wheel. As he squeezed by, he shook his head with contempt. Jittery and angry, Davis backed onto the intersecting street, where another horn warned him as he squealed away in the right direction. "Rednecks!" he shouted into the hot air inside the car.

The word surprised him, and he wondered for a moment if he had really said it. But there it was, the aftertaste still in his mouth. Like it or not, these were his people, and he had often defended their nobility whenever the stereotype ambled into conversation, that slack-jawed, barefooted caricature. Amazing how such biases hold on, even in the face of the so-called New South, with its skyscrapers and commerce. Rednecks marry their cousins and get dumber with each generation, devolving into something simian. Why, they'd just as soon shoot you as look at you, the Gomers and Goobers and Jethros and Davises. If you call someone in your home Uncle Daddy, you're probably a redneck. Even Ben Blau would think twice before telling that joke. But then he was family. You can poke fun if you're a blood member. His father had once laughed and said to him, "You're one of society's worst nightmares, a redneck with a Ph.D."

He found a street that went through in the right direction and followed it to a bluff at the edge of town, one of his favorite places, a spot left vacant by some quirk of zoning, a little promontory with a view of the traffic on Riverside Drive and the Cumberland River beyond. When he had found it years ago, it seemed secret and pristine. Now, he stepped from the car onto a path of bare dirt, the surrounding brush strewn with beer cans and cigarette butts. Near the edge of the bluff, a large spot had been wallowed in the weeds, as if a huge animal had slept there. Likely high school kids with a blanket.

Below him, the traffic strung out, following the river, making a noise like wind in tall cedars. He had brought his mother here once, in the first year after his father died, thinking she would find it calming. Instead, she looked out over the cars and the tops of the franchise stores and said, "What a mess." Nothing whimsical or sentimental—what she would call "sappy"—could penetrate her practical, direct approach to life. No jewelry, no makeup, no interest in the household pets. When Tippy grew so old he couldn't walk without dragging his rear quarters, Davis's mother was the one who put the poor dog out of his misery, loading him into the trunk of the car for a last trip to the vet's, saying to Davis, "Come on, boy, quit bawling. It's just a dog."

"Yeah, what a mess," he reflected now, looking out over the river into a brown line of trees that would soon be in full bud. Always skeptical of his mother's blunt simplicity, he was nevertheless a little envious of it. What would she say right now to put everything into plain perspective?

"Look, kid, you've gotta deal with reality. People die. I'm dead and there's no changing that, so pick up and go on. You'll die, too. Everybody dies."

But death has shock waves. What about those? What about the ground shaking underneath your feet while you try to go on? What about the little piece of who you are that dies with another person and can't ever be retrieved?

"You know, Davis, when people talk about death they get all squidgy. They start saying things you never hear them say any other time—goofy, mushy stuff. It's better to put your trust in the Lord and then not worry. What's the point anyway?"

Put your trust in the Lord. That, too, was ironic. Raised a Southern Baptist, she had attended church regularly when Davis was a child but had stopped going once he reached his mid-teens, convinced she'd done her duty. Belief, for her, wasn't a matter of faith but of common sense. "I don't know enough not to believe," she once said. "Anyhow, what can it hurt? Might even pay off in the long run."

The sun was warm on Davis's face as he lay back on the brittle weeds and closed his eyes. "Must be close to eleven," he guessed, resisting the urge to look at his watch. The light through his eyelids was an orange dome, "the color of the sky on another planet," he thought, watching a deeper red seep through and then become a numbing, crimson blackness.

In the blood-dark of his slumber, a question resonated: "What is nothing? Come on, think hard, Davis. What is nothing?"

"Gotta be a trick question," Davis reasoned, studying the blank page in front of him. He had to write something or he would fail, but writing something would subvert the question, which itself wasn't written down but was ringing in the air as if he had asked it himself. Looking around, he could see no one else, only empty desks. "Maybe the right answer is to hand in the page with nothing on it. That's it! With *nothing* on it!" But then he was writing, "Nothing is no thing, the absence of thingness. Since the mind is a thing, it can't conceive its own absence. Therefore, nothing doesn't exist."

"Shit! A double negative. Gotta be the wrong answer." And then the words he had written began to look like squiggles, like a child's mimicry of language, and a hole opened up somewhere in the center of his chest and he fell into himself, into nothing, nothing, no thing.

"Oh, God!" he screamed, sitting straight up, breathless and damp with sweat. For a moment, he didn't know where he was, his blood rushing like the traffic below. He looked at his watch. Eleven-thirty. He had been asleep for at least half an hour. Stumbling to his feet, he brushed the debris from his pants and ran a hand through his hair to pull out a dried weed stem. He yanked his shirttail free and fanned it, trying to circulate air underneath as he walked back to the car.

Vertigo was the name he gave these episodes, because he

had to call them something, even though he never talked about them with anyone. They had plagued him since childhood, when he would start to plummet just before falling asleep and have to sit up and clutch something solid to keep from losing himself. It was as if he might really go over the edge, the final edge. Sometimes he figured that he should give in to the sensation, that yielding to it might be the way to conquer it, but he lacked the courage. He had even armed himself with some reassuring terminology—Dark Night of the Soul—and a maxim that was paradoxical and therefore wonderfully suited to his absurd problem—"The way down is the way up." But in the face of that yawning chasm, which seemed simultaneously inside and outside him, such philosophical nets were pathetically small.

"The answering abyss," he thought as he gripped the warm door handle of the car, liking the sound of the words, feeling they explained something, though he couldn't be sure what.

Checking his face in the mirror, he tried to smooth his hair where it had been flattened during his nap, then shook his head vigorously and made a growling noise to shake off the self-loathing he felt coming on. His throat was lacquered—by the sun, he reasoned, shoving aside the knowledge of thirst as a symptom of very high blood sugar. Thinking of something cold to drink, he turned in the direction of Two Rivers Mall at the bottom of the hill, the mall that had killed downtown Clarksville and was now slowly dying itself as a newer commercial development on the other side of town lured people away.

The parking lot that had been a demolition derby of cars competing for space was now so empty Davis pulled into a slot ten yards from the main door. Once inside, he watched the young woman at the Orange Julius counter crack an egg into a cup, blend it, and then hand the concoction to an old man in a

FORGET, HELL! cap with a cartoon Confederate brandishing a sword.

"A large diet cola," he said when the clerk's eyes rolled toward him.

He chose a bench in the center of the mall, so he could watch the few customers stroll in and out of stores. Occasionally, small groups of older women squeaked by in walking shoes, arms neatly bent, uppercutting the air. Less than four months ago, he had wandered from window to window here, trying to find a Christmas present for his mother, whose no-frills lifestyle made gifts difficult. More than once, she had returned a bathrobe or a pair of house slippers, saying, "I don't need anything this nice. Besides, I can have two for what you paid."

In desperation, he had bought a bathroom set: hand towel, bath towel, washcloth, toilet-seat cover, and bath rug, all green. Pulling on the straw in his soft drink, he tried to remember if those were the ones he had seen in the bathroom that morning.

"Davis?" a voice asked over his shoulder. "Davis Banks?"

Turning around, he saw a middle-aged woman in a tailored tan suit smiling down at him. "It's Ann Louise, Ann Louise Wilson. You don't remember me, do you?"

Until he heard the name, Davis didn't remember, but then Ann Louise's face from high school became visible behind the older one he hadn't recognized.

"Ann Louise! Of course I remember you," he insisted, watching both faces merge.

"Don't tell me you've finally moved back."

"No. No . . . I'm here on personal business. My mother just died." Once more, Davis's honesty took him off guard.

Ann Louise stood for a moment, then sat down on the bench, her shoulder bag between them.

"I lost my parents a few years ago," she said. "It's not easy, is it?" Slipping the strap off her shoulder, Ann Louise moved the bag to her other side.

"No." Davis felt distant.

"I'm on my lunch break. Headed for the salad bar at Morrison's."

Davis stood and looked at his watch.

"In a hurry?"

"No. Just don't want to make you late."

"That your lunch?" she asked, pointing to the soft-drink cup.

"Uh, no. I'm supposed to eat later with my relatives. You know how they pile on the food when someone dies."

"Then you can talk to me while I eat," she said, standing quickly and looking directly into Davis's eyes.

They walked without speaking into the deep-fried smell of Morrison's Cafeteria, and Ann Louise slid a tray along the silver bars that passed before steaming heaps of food. A simple gesture would produce a bowl of pinto beans or a plate of crumbly chicken, and Davis watched as everyone around him pointed at almost everything, some of them needing two trays to hold the bowls and plates.

"This must be the only place in the mall that isn't about to go under."

"People have to eat," Ann Louise responded, deciding on the garden-fresh salad.

Once they were seated, Davis silently created interlocking wet rings on the tabletop with the bottom of his water glass, until he grew self-conscious and said, "So, where do you work?"

"I'm a . . ." Ann Louise started, then held up her hand, forefinger extended, to mark her place in the conversation while she swallowed. "I'm a detective," she said, dabbing the corners of her mouth with her napkin. "Clarksville Police Department."

Davis felt himself slipping into Ben Blau mode. A detective, right. He almost asked to see her badge or gun but said only, "Really?"

"No, I just say that to make people think I'm capable of holding down a tough job and to scare away the creeps. I'm actually a napkin folder at the Stagecoach Inn."

"Sorry. Did I sound that astonished?"

Ann Louise smiled faintly and said, "It's all right. I get the wide-eyed treatment a lot. Can't say I'm used to it, but it doesn't surprise me anymore."

"How did you become a detective?"

Drawing in a deep breath, Ann Louise gave what sounded like a stock recitation of facts: "Started out in law school. Didn't like it. Switched to law enforcement. Spent eight years in a squad car. Got promoted." After she finished, she made a mock bow from the waist.

Ignoring the sarcasm, Davis followed with another question. "What's your area of expertise?"

"Homicide."

"Are there enough murders in Clarksville to keep you busy?"

"I don't remember you as a smart-ass, but you're doing a good impression of one right now."

For the first time, Davis noticed the color of Ann Louise's eyes, green-gold, and the way her brown hair caught the light in a soft curve on each side of her face. He wanted to start over, to call 911 and ask for her: "Man needs assistance in Two Rivers Mall."

"Davis. Davis." Her voice echoed across a void, as if he were dead or dying and she was trying to call him back. He waited for her to ask, "Who did this to you?" But she just kept saying his name.

"Uh, look, I've got to go," he said, stumbling to his feet. His body was almost too heavy to move, or the air itself had become thicker. Signs of dangerously high blood sugar. Why hadn't he checked when the insatiable thirst came on? Could be off the scale by now. When he reached the car and dropped the keys while getting inside, he realized Ann Louise had followed him.

She picked up the keys and held on to them. "You on something?" she asked, sounding like a cop.

Davis was fumbling with his diabetic kit, trying to get his blood sugar meter and the insulin he knew he would need. Without answering Ann Louise's question, he pricked a finger and placed a drop of blood on a strip he inserted into the small meter. In less than a minute, the number 573 appeared in the little window. "Holy shit!"

"What's wrong?" Ann Louise asked, his tension infecting her.

"I'm a damned diabetic, that's what's wrong." Already, he was drawing insulin into a syringe and swabbing a spot on his stomach. "Ten units ought to do it," he calculated aloud, forgetting about Ann Louise as he jabbed the needle in and thumbed the plunger. When she insisted that he needed a doctor, he laughed and said, "Actually, I need a pancreas."

"Move over," she ordered, one foot already edging him away from the driver's side. "You're not in any condition to drive." Or did she say, "Your condition is driving me in"? He couldn't be sure as he slumped to his right and closed his eyes. Such a sweet peacefulness, green-gold and darkening.

Her question "How long do these spells usually last?" roused Davis from his stupor, though the air still felt like pudding.

"Spells?" he asked, looking about him at a strange neighborhood.

"Come on, better get you inside." Now she was opening the car door on his side and grasping his left forearm and elbow.

"You gonna cuff me?" He laughed.

The last thing he remembered was the door, a darkened room, a bed. Then he was deep in the chocolate dark, his mind a dropped jigsaw of images.

·

Static chatter. Snippets of griffin-speak. And he snapped awake. "Who's there?" he challenged, drawing his legs toward him and backing against the headboard of the bed.

Then Ann Louise's face became visible as she turned on a lamp. The voices kept shrilling from a two-way radio lying on the foot of the bed until she turned it off, saying, "They can get along without me for half an hour."

Davis felt himself struggling to assemble the pieces—the woman, the room, the voices. Tentatively, he said, "Ann Louise . . ."

"You're at my place. You've been sleeping for over two hours, which makes it nearly three P.M." She tipped her wrist toward the lamplight to check her watch. "Quarter till, to be exact."

Davis looked around the room. Except for the bed, a night table and lamp, it was empty. No pictures on the walls, no dresser or bureau. At one end, a closet door stood half open. "This what you cops call a safe house?"

Ann Louise laughed as she sat on the end of the bed. "Safe enough. It's my house."

Davis could feel her weight through the coils in the box springs and mattress as she shifted to look more directly at him. "Right. I remember you said that a minute ago," he said.

"Is this what they call a diabetic reaction?"

The question made Davis feel weary. How to explain diabetes to someone who knows nothing about it? "No, not a reaction. It's the opposite, in fact."

When Davis said nothing else, Ann Louise leaned toward him. "I don't get it."

"Okay. A reaction involves too much insulin. What happened to me at the mall was the result of too much sugar and not enough insulin."

"Is it dangerous? I mean, could you die?"

"It would take a few days with high blood sugar. Much faster with insulin shock."

"Then why didn't you let me call a doctor?"

"All I needed was a shot of insulin, and I got that. Now I'm fine, as you can see."

"You don't look so great to me."

"Well, you look terrific from where I'm sitting."

They fell silent. Ann Louise rose quickly and was nearly out of the room when she remembered her radio and turned back. "Look, stay as long as you like. Your car's parked out front." Then she was gone.

In the bathroom, Davis splashed water on his face and reached for a towel. It was damp. He buried his face in it, slowly inhaling the scent of Ann Louise's soap. Then he looked up at himself in the mirror and said, "Pervert."

He walked through the small house, each room empty or stacked with unpacked boxes. In the living room, a single recliner faced a small television. It was not so much a room for living as for waiting, somehow personal despite its sparse decor. No plants, no knickknacks. Nothing on the walls. As he backed out and pulled the door toward him, her soap-scent swarmed his head.

CHAPTER 5

Davis got to Uncle Oscar and Aunt Goldie's around five-thirty. As he pulled into their driveway, the commotion began—half a dozen cousins spilling onto the front porch and lawn. Leading them, wringing her hands in her flowered apron, was Goldie. All hips and thighs, she seemed to be spreading slowly back into the earth, her narrow shoulders topped by a little head that bobbled from side to side as if it needed tightening at the neck.

"Where in the world you been? I got so frantic I sent Gaylon to your mama's house to see if you was all right."

Looking slightly amused by the whole scene and grateful to be only on the fringes of it, Gaylon, the lanky teenage son of a cousin, said, "The house was all shut up, so I thumped on the windows and blew my horn real loud. Then I seen the car was gone."

"See," Goldie said emphatically. "We was all worried."

Davis heard himself say he had driven out into the country and gotten lost. "Ended up having lunch with an old couple named Scofield or Sheffield. Never could quite make out the name. Real nice folks."

"Ain't nobody with neither of them names around here, boy. You must've got yourself real lost," Uncle Oscar said with a sidelong regard.

"Well, come on in, come on in. There's still food on the table," said Aunt Goldie as she scurried everyone toward the house, her square-heeled shoes pecking the sidewalk. "Whatever you had at that other place can't compare with family cooking."

Davis was about to say the Scofield/Sheffields were somebody's family, when he realized Aunt Goldie was standing beside a chair at the table with her spoon dipped into a bowl brimming with crowder peas. "Well, do you or don't you?" she asked.

"Uh, yes, I do," said Davis, abruptly brought back. He unfolded a turquoise paper napkin as he sat down.

Aunt Goldie nudged turnip greens, beef roast, gravy, and green beans onto his crowded plate. Meals at her house were modeled on excess—too much of everything, including at least three different kinds of potatoes—stewed, mashed, and fried.

Some of the second cousins carried off more helpings of the greens and crowders from the table, even though they had already eaten. The adults pulled up chairs and studied Davis as he broke off small pieces of his corn bread.

"How was your trip?" asked Gaylon, lifting a glass of iced tea.

His mouth full, Davis could only nod and make an "unnh"

sound. After swallowing, he said, "I hate flying, though. Always seem to sit next to someone with a big tale to tell."

The dining room opened directly onto the living room, and Davis could see still other cousins and their children on the sofa and chairs. Except for the smallest, who were playing with a toy dump truck and plastic soldiers on the carpet, everyone looked expectantly at him, as if he might offer up a revelation or confession. Feeling his throat tighten under the scrutiny, he put down his fork and said, "I can't eat another bite."

"But you hardly ate nothing," protested Aunt Goldie. "You always used to like my cooking."

Davis considered telling her that he shouldn't be eating anything without knowing his blood sugar level and taking insulin. But as if reading his mind, Aunt Goldie slid a piece of pecan pie toward him, saying, "I know you ain't supposed to eat sweets, but just have a little bitty taste."

Knowing resistance would make things worse, Davis took a bite and rolled his eyes upward in pretend pleasure when he felt the cold tines of the fork on his tongue. Silently, he calculated the insulin he would need to counteract the dense sweetness.

"Coffee?" someone asked from the kitchen, but Davis flagged her off with his left hand while wiping his mouth with the napkin in his right.

"Oughta come home more often," chided Uncle Oscar, "get to know these cousins a yours a little better."

Davis scooted his chair away from the table, ignoring him. Aunt Goldie and the women cleared away the bowls and put foil over the pie. When Davis offered to help, they shushed him into the living room where a grubby toddler wobbled up with candy extended in the palm of his hand and pressed the chocolate goo into the leg of Davis's pants, saying, "Me got, galala."

"Cody!" yelled one of his cousins. "Now look what you done to the man's pretty pants. You bad boy! Bad, bad boy! Tell him you're sorry."

"It's okay," Davis said with a clear tone of insincerity. "It'll wash out," but he couldn't imagine how. He had brought very little to wear and needed these trousers.

Then came Aunt Goldie with a damp cloth and a bottle of dish detergent. She knelt and rubbed hard at the stain while Davis looked down into her teased, thinning hair. The imprint of the tiny palm began to fade, but the stain was twice its original size.

Davis sat down next to Gaylon, who had moved from the kitchen to the sofa. Trying to make small talk, Davis asked, "What kind of car do you have?"

"Ain't a car; it's a truck," Gaylon replied. "A Ford. Parked right in fronta the house." Gaylon pointed toward the picture window and across the short lawn to a forest-green truck sitting so high on its springs it seemed to be levitating.

Aunt Goldie plopped down between them and, hanging her arm around Davis's shoulders, said, "It's hard, ain't it, darlin'?"

Davis shifted slightly to loosen her hug.

"Don't forget, I've lost my sister," Goldie said, her voice taking on the dolorous tone of a mourner. "Of course, losing your mama is harder, I know."

It was one of Aunt Goldie's patented explosive devices. Agree with her and she would take offense at having her own grief belittled. Disagree and get the lecture about mothers and sons and filial responsibility.

"We're all in a lot of pain," Davis said, fingering the damp spot on his trouser leg. Aunt Goldie's response was obliterated by a blare from the television.

"Sorry," Uncle Oscar said, "I mashed the sound instead of

the channel changer." He settled back in his recliner and clicked rapidly, creating a montage of car chases, toothpaste, wild animals, game shows, and exercise equipment.

Aunt Goldie rose and went back into the kitchen, where she and Cody's mother began washing dishes. Their voices were fractured by the clatter of silverware and pots, but Davis was certain they were talking about him, and he wished he could take Uncle Oscar's remote control and raise the volume of their conversation.

At one end of the living room, a reproduction of *The Last Supper* hung above a table where a dozen wide-eyed figurines were assembled—mostly deer and bunnies—grazing the lace-edged table runner. Directly above the television was a banjo clock, complete with strings, Oscar's proudest creation. Its filigree hands blurred from a distance, making it impossible to tell the exact time. And photographs hung everywhere else, most of them black-and-white Olan Mills portraits taken in hotel rooms in the early sixties, backdrops of mountains and meadows. Davis studied one of Goldie and Oscar seated shoulder to shoulder like strangers on a bus.

"So why ain't you married?" Gaylon asked, rubbing the knees of his jeans, his question coming from somewhere near the outer perimeter of the known universe.

Clearing his throat, Davis responded, "I was once."

"What happened?" Gaylon persisted.

"Quit your prying, boy," called Aunt Goldie, demonstrating her remarkable hearing and her unconscious command of the ironic. No one meddled more in other people's lives than Aunt Goldie.

"Sorry." Gaylon sulked as he slid a little further toward his end of the sofa and propped his right leg on his left knee, clasping his foot with both hands and pulling it toward him as if he were preparing to perform a contortionist's trick.

"That's okay," Davis reassured him. "I got divorced because things just didn't work out."

That was an understatement. He had known before the ceremony, before he showed up one evening with a grin on his face and an engagement ring in his pocket, that they would never make it together. HOMETOWN BOY AND GIRL GET MARRIED. That could have been the newspaper headline, with the subhead LOCALS GIVE POOR ODDS FOR COUPLE. They had had nothing in common except the need to be married. Before the first year was up, they had run out of things to say to each other and communicated in a nonverbal code. Davis would hold up the car keys and jingle them as he turned the doorknob, and Linda would swivel from the television long enough to nod, her signal that she knew he was going somewhere but she didn't care where.

Gaylon was clearly brooding, but he brightened when Davis punched him on the arm and said, "Don't worry, cuz. I don't mind. Let's look at that truck of yours."

Davis had no real interest in the vehicle but needed to get outside, to clear his head of the babble. Gaylon lifted the hood, licked his finger, and rubbed at a smudge on one of the chrome valve covers. Not knowing what to say, Davis exclaimed, "Pretty neat," then tried to cover his ignorance and lack of interest by asking a question. "How fast have you run her?"

Gaylon shuffled his feet in the gravel. "I'm a pretty safe driver."

"Yeah, but just between you and me, what have you seen on the speedometer?"

"Seen the needle buried."

"Whatta you figure—one-twenty, one-twenty-five?"

"Felt more like one-fifty. Tires plain floated over low places in the road."

Davis was quiet, recalling his own teenage recklessness.

Afraid of nothing. Definitely not of death. He closed his eyes and remembered how it was, the wind ripping past, the pavement coming up faster than film rewinding. "What'd it feel like?" he asked Gaylon.

"Didn't feel like nothin'."

"Was it fun?"

"Just somethin' to do. You know."

Davis definitely knew the bravado, the breathlessness as the car slowed down and came back into control, the weakness in his arms and knees. "Let's take her out."

"You mean now?"

"Sure, why not? Let's see what she'll do."

"Uh, I don't know if we should."

"It's your truck, isn't it? Just tell your mama you and I are gonna take a spin."

When Gaylon came back, Davis was sitting behind the wheel, his hand extended for the keys. Gaylon looked uncertain but dropped them into Davis's palm. "Square one's the ignition," he said.

"Still good pavement out in the direction of Trenton?" Davis asked, jerking away from the curb, unused to a clutch and manual shift. He took Gaylon's silence as assent and headed north into Kentucky. When they got beyond the franchises and bunched traffic, he increased the speed. Eighty in no time. Gaylon was tipped so he could see the speedometer but kept glancing up through the windshield.

"Good, straight stretch up here somewhere," Davis said, pressing harder on the accelerator. One hundred. One-ten. When the needle disappeared beyond the one-twenty mark, he shouted to Gaylon, "Close your eyes."

"What?" Gaylon's voice was tight with fear.

"Close your eyes. I'm closing mine."

"You crazy?" Gaylon sat upright in his seat and seemed

about to pray. Davis closed his eyes and held the wheel firm, feeling the hard vibration along his arms and down his spine. The speed was purified by the absence of vision, a heart-rush into the blackout, a diabetic plunge without the loss of consciousness.

"Whee-ha!" screamed Davis, opening his eyes just in time to see Gaylon reaching for the wheel. "Don't do that! You'll jerk us off the road!"

Gaylon was panting, and his legs were drawn up against the seat. "Stop! Stop!" he yelled, until Davis slowed and pulled onto the shoulder. While the truck was still rolling, Gaylon jumped out, bounded the ditch, and fell forward onto the embankment. Rolling over, he sat up, both hands gripping the earth at his sides, his eyes fixed on Davis, the look of the blind in them.

"First time you've gone that fast, isn't it?" Davis asked from the opposite side of the ditch. Gaylon gulped, trying to get enough air. "Isn't it?" Still no answer. "First rule of lying," Davis said, leaping the ditch and standing over Gaylon, "is never tell a lie that can be challenged on the spot. Doesn't matter if people think you might be lying, just don't give them a chance to prove you are."

"You're fucking crazy, man," Gaylon said, his voice small and tense.

Davis sat down in the weeds beside him. "Second rule is build a lie partly on the truth, or else make it so big and wild it's obviously a lie, but one everyone wants to believe."

"Why are you telling me this shit? Give me the keys, man. I don't have to take this shit."

"Gaylon, 'shit' is not the original cosmic word."

"I don't know what you're talking about. This is weird."

"Listen. I'm trying to let you in on something most people

never figure out. Life is built on lies. Memory is a lie, so the past is a lie. You understand?"

Gaylon picked sticktights from his socks and said, "That's stupid. If something happens, it happens."

"Yes, but how you remember it will be different from the way anybody else remembers it. Memory bends things. Haven't you ever had an argument with someone over something you both saw or did? You have one version and the other guy has another?"

"Sure, but that don't change what happened."

"No? Well, answer a simple question. Did I close my eyes at a hundred and twenty miles an hour?"

"I don't know."

"You were there. I know you didn't close yours, so you must have noticed what I was doing. Did I close them?"

"Yeah, okay, you closed them."

"For how long?"

"This is stupid, man. How'm I supposed to know?"

"You're supposed to know because you were there, on that front seat with me. How long?"

When Gaylon refused to answer, Davis said, "Must have had 'em clenched tight for at least fifteen seconds, maybe twenty."

"No way!"

"But you said you didn't know."

"I know nobody could hold a truck on the road for that long with his eyes closed."

"I did. And do you know what it felt like? Like holding your breath underwater. Can you prove I didn't do it?"

"Let's go back. Gimme the keys."

Davis jumped the ditch and then tossed the keys to Gaylon as he stood up, testing his knees. Then, while Gaylon watched,

Davis took a quarter from his pocket and placed it on the shoulder of the road.

"What'd you do that for?"

"Ever find a quarter or a dime?"

"Sure, who hasn't?"

"Made you feel lucky, didn't it? Made you sure whatever had been wrong was about to change. Well, I drop coins so people can find them and get that rush. Makes me feel good."

"That's a lie, ain't it?"

"You just saw me drop a quarter here for the next hitch-hiker to find, and I told you why I did it. Can you prove I'm lying?"

On the way back, Gaylon said nothing and kept well within the speed limit. He looked straight ahead and, when parked in front of his grandparents' house, got out and walked off down the street. Davis went inside.

"Have a nice drive?" asked one of the cousins.

"Sure did. Beautiful day to take in the countryside."

"Where's Gaylon?" someone asked.

"I think he's fiddling around with his truck. You know how teenage boys are." Popping around the corner into the kitchen, where his aunt sat at a small table drinking coffee with her oldest daughter, Davis said, "Gotta go. Thanks for the meal." Treena, her name was Treena, Gaylon's mother. "Good to see you, Treena," he said, glad to have remembered in time. Then he spun and was out the front door before Goldie could stall him, but he heard her wail of complaint mixed with the blare of the television. Neither roused Oscar from his sleep.

When he got into the car, Davis had no destination in mind but found himself driving to Greenwood Cemetery, his father's final resting place. Known at one time as a great spot for lovers to park, Greenwood now had a bold sign at the entrance—CLOSED AT SUNDOWN—and a heavy chain ready to join the low stone pillars of the gate. Davis steered under maples and oaks, past ancient grave markers, and saluted the ornate Confederate monument as he wound by on his way to the newer section where the stones were flush with the ground for easy mowing.

Rolling to a stop, he could hear the whir of pinwheels on the mound of a child. At the spot where his father was buried, a yellow backhoe sat, its scoop knuckling the grass. As he walked toward it, he realized his mother's grave had already been dug, red earth piled at one end of a rectangular hole. The late-afternoon sunlight cast an angular shadow across the opening, a door ajar. Davis sat and dangled his feet in the grave, feeling the cool air around his ankles. "Even cooler at the bottom," he thought, easing himself over the ragged edge, surprised by the distance of the drop. Landing awkwardly, he struck his shoulder on one of the earthen sides but kept his balance and remained standing. Fully extending his arms above his head, he could see the sunlight on his hands and wrists. The rest of him was in shadow, and when he lowered his arms, he felt his heart quicken and noticed how the earth deadened the sound of his breath.

"So this is where Mama will spend eternity," he said, his voice sounding stoppered and strange.

Lying down to feel the exact position she would be in, Davis held himself as still as possible and studied the slab of blue above him, trying to think of nothing. But he was thinking of his father, not six feet under but inches to his right, a thin wall of dirt between them. "Hello, Dad," he said, placing a hand on the vertical wall, only it wasn't earth or stone he felt. It was something else—fabric, stiff as canvas. Afraid to move, he left his hand there, thinking about the coffin and the impossibility of touching his father. "Can't be. Cannot be." And as he insisted that he couldn't be doing what he was doing, he gripped the cloth and pulled something through the earth. At first it seemed like a practical joke, bones in a sleeve. Death's hand extended in greeting. A human arm. His father's arm. Then Davis was on his feet, trying to climb out of the grave, the earth crumbling down around him, the light completely gone now from the rim of the opening. But the harder he climbed, the less progress he made, a hoarse sound coming now from his own throat, coming with each breath, the whoosh of a blade, and he could feel the earth in his hair, under his nails; he could taste it, and it fell into his lashes and blinked his eyes, and he fell back down.

From somewhere, he heard a whistle, a distant, sliding note, and he knew someone was calling a dog among the headstones. Knowing this, he began to breathe with less effort and slumped into a crouch, forced himself to imagine the dog nosing his way among the graves, flushing robins and rabbits. Holding the dog in mind, he began to climb, considering its name as he jabbed his toes into the grave wall for footing. "Jack or Buck or Princess," he thought, "maybe Lady or Lucy," and then he rolled himself over the rim and onto the swooning sod of his father's grave. The sky was still bright, and the sunlight yellowed the treetops all around, but the shadow-tide had risen and he could almost hear, as he lay on the darkening grass, the night coming in like a huge breaker.

CHAPTER 6

FINDING ANN LOUISE's house was harder than Davis imagined. Too many new subdivisions. Dozens of dead-end streets with circular turnarounds. And he wasn't sure he would recognize the place in the dark. Embarrassing to admit he was lost in his own hometown, so when a random turn placed him on one of the old thoroughfares, he was relieved. At least he could go home and phone Ann Louise. She was a cop. She would know where to begin. "The bastards at Berkley's!" Davis thought of them switching coffins at graveside after everyone had left, putting his father in a plain box or maybe just dumping him into the hole.

When he stepped into his mother's house and switched on

the overhead light, he saw how filthy he was. He left a little dune of dirt on the entryway rug when he took off his shoes, and could feel more soil inside his socks, between his toes, as he took long strides across the carpet. No Ann Louise Wilson in the phone book, but A.L. had to be the right one. Windom Lane, wherever that was. After five rings, an answering machine picked up, Ann Louise's voice saying simply, "Please leave a message."

"Ah, Davis. This is Davis Banks. I need your advice about something. I'll try again later." He sounded stupid and wished he could erase himself. Maybe he should call back and leave a better message, but he might do even worse. When the machine beeped, he realized it had been recording dead air as he held the phone, the emptiness of the open grave. Zero acoustics. Forcing a yawn, Davis made his ears pop, trying to return to level ground; but the house itself seemed sunken in sand, drifts above the roofline, obliteration.

Imagine the highway's sweet fatigue, hour upon hour of broken center line, tires shushing, wind buffeting the car like a storm of petals. The brain says, "Stay awake," but the body has its own urges. The brain says, "Stay awake or die," but the body is half in love with death and hears the lovely interval between words, the breathless stops. So it is when the limbs go under, heavy with sugar, glazed and ponderous, the blood slowed to syrup. Davis lay on the floor, knowing he needed insulin, the word itself sounding in his brain like the twilight call of the whippoorwill. The darkening field and the darker woods. Whippoorwill. Insulin.

"Did you know I could commit suicide with five pounds of Swiss chocolate?" Rim shot. No laughter. "That is, if I wanted to go out in style. Or I could get down and dirty with a case of Little Debbie Snack Cakes." No sound in the dim room, just Davis thumping the microphone. "Hello. Anybody there?" Electronic feedback, piercing screel. "Hello." And then a thumping, knocking. Siren. Ambulance on the way. Knocking. "Hello." And Davis rose from the swamp of himself, hearing the whine of the telephone, off the hook, and someone pounding at the front door.

"Davis. Davis. Are you in there?" It was Ann Louise, her fist raised to bang the door again, when Davis opened it. "What happened to you?" she asked, eyeing his dirty shirt and pants.

"Just a minute," he said, turning back into the room.

"Davis?" Ann Louise called after him, standing in the entryway next to his shoes. The phone pulsed, insistent. "Are you all right?"

In the bathroom's spitting fluorescence, Davis injected himself. No point in taking a reading to prove what he already knew: sugar dangerously high. No need to estimate the insulin dosage. A dozen units would be just a beginning. Coming down from such heights was slower than climbing. Adjusting to the different altitudes, needle by needle. Drop too quickly and the bottom comes up to kiss you. "Can't keep letting this happen," he thought, but another voice, more weary, asked, "What's the difference?" His spine still held the grave's cool press of earth.

"Davis," Ann Louise insisted, saying his name as if it were an imperative. "What's going on here? I got a strange message on my machine and couldn't call you back because your phone was off the hook. Now you won't answer me, but you seem to be having a pretty good conversation with yourself."

Davis hadn't realized he was speaking instead of thinking. "What'd I say?"

"Look, you need medical attention."

"How much do you know about diabetes?" Davis challenged.

"I know sometimes a person having an insulin reaction may appear to be drunk."

"And that's it? The full extent of your knowledge?"

The derisive tone in Davis's voice made Ann Louise bristle. "I'm a cop, not a doctor."

"Just trust me on this, okay?" Davis insisted. "I don't need anything but the insulin I just took."

"This is the way you live your life? Falling asleep and waking up just in time to shoot up some insulin?"

"That's about right." Davis waved a hand from side to side, metronome motion. "Say one end of the wave is high and the other end is low. Where you want to be is somewhere in the middle." He kept up the monotonous movement, then asked, "How much of the time is my hand in the middle?" When Ann Louise shrugged, he said, "Never. It's always rising or falling."

"What you're saying is, you're never all right."

Davis stopped moving his hand but didn't respond, thinking the question should answer itself. Leaning over the sink and looking into the mirror as he spoke, he said, "I need your advice."

"You don't strike me as someone who takes advice." Ann Louise crossed her arms as if evaluating him.

"What can a person do if he discovers an undertaker has ripped him off?"

"Hire a lawyer, I guess."

"But what if it happened eight years ago, and the only way to prove it is to exhume a body?"

"Exactly what are we talking about here?"

As Davis recounted his visit to the cemetery and what he had found, her mood changed from irritation to excitement. "We've got to go have a look," she said.

"In the dark?" Davis protested. "Anyway, the cemetery's closed by now."

"Come on. You don't have to go in. Just point me in the right direction so I can find the grave."

Too groggy to argue, Davis picked up his shoes and carried them out the front door. Sitting on the steps, he laced them as Ann Louise walked partway to her car and then back, pacing the lawn in her nylon running suit as if warming up for the long miles. Each step whispered "now," and the streetlight shining on the navy fabric made her look slickery and fast.

Driving to the cemetery, she leaned forward as though stretching for the finish line, as though she could get there before the car. Because the chain at the entrance of Greenwood blocked the road, Ann Louise pulled over near the wall, so close that Davis couldn't open the door and had to slide across to get out on the driver's side. She had already stepped over the chain and was vanishing in the dark when he called her name. The sound of it surprised him, an invocation in this place of the dead. No response. When he called a second time, a beam of light swung toward him, pulling him down the narrow lane. Until Ann Louise spoke, he would have sworn the light had lifted him several feet above the ground. "Don't just stand there; come on and show me the grave." Her voice could have been coming from the other side of a door.

When her flashlight beam found the yellow backhoe, Ann Louise outpaced Davis and was watching the small circle flatten and dim at the bottom of the grave when he walked up beside her. "Can't see anything from here," she said, sitting and then dropping over the edge.

"Dark as the grave down there," Davis wisecracked.

Ann Louise said nothing as she followed the light that bobbled in front of her like a terrier on a leash. End to end. Corner to corner. Now and then she stooped. Davis could hardly see her, just the light and a shape that might be anyone. Any body.

"See anything yet?" He leaned as far over the edge as he

could, letting his voice fall like a fistful of dirt. Then the light went out. "Ann Louise? You all right?" Nothing. "Don't play games, Ann Louise!" On his stomach now, his face level with the edge, he was about to scream into the pit when he realized Ann Louise was immediately below him, looking up.

"Who's playing games?" she said, her face a pale, floating oval.

"Why'd you turn off the light?" Davis barely whispered.

"Why'd you bring me out here?"

"Hey, it wasn't my idea to come out here in the middle of the night. That was Detective Wilson's mission, as I recall."

"There's no arm down here, Davis."

"Come on. I didn't make it up. There was a sleeve with bones in it."

"You want to look for yourself?"

Davis began to lift himself, thinking he would show Ann Louise exactly where it was, but then flattened out again and reached down a hand, saying, "Here, grab hold." One tug and she had her elbows over the edge.

"I can make it," she insisted, holding still until he released her arm. In what seemed a single motion, she was out and sitting on the grass. Davis lay facedown, watching the darkness in the grave well up and spill over. "Don't sulk," Ann Louise said, stretching "sulk" to two syllables. "Coons probably got it."

The explanation was something he might devise to sustain one of his lies. The other possibilities blinked in his mind like flash cards: Kids found it and took it as a secret relic; someone saw him scramble from the grave and made off with the arm after he left; his father reached through the dirt and retrieved the detached part of himself; no arm ever existed except in his imagination. The last option made him uneasy. Had he perfected the lie so well he could trick himself? Rolling over and sitting up next to Ann Louise, he asked, "Do you believe in the truth?"

She was silent for so long that Davis closed his eyes and imagined she had disappeared. "I believe in the facts," she said finally, "just the facts," her voice taking on the staccato pattern of Sergeant Joe Friday.

"I'm serious."

"So am I. The facts don't lie, so they're as close to the truth as you can get."

"But what if you've got two sets of facts—I saw a body part in that grave and you didn't? Where's the truth?"

"Come on, Davis. Be logical. These facts don't cancel each other. Besides, I've got another fact right here." Extending her clenched hand palm down, she said, "Take it."

Davis didn't move, thinking it was some kind of joke. "It's not a worm, is it?"

Ann Louise laughed. "Just go ahead and take it."

When Davis opened his hand, Ann Louise placed hers on it and slowly opened her fingers. Sensation of a caress, soft hover of fingers over his wrist, where the pulse quickened. He was leaning toward her, thinking of her green-gold eyes, when she withdrew her hand and his spontaneously closed around what she had given him, something small and solid. A ring. "Does this mean we're going steady?" he asked clumsily.

Without answering, Ann Louise handed him her flashlight. In the yellowish light, the ring looked like a museum piece, a clunky chunk of gold with a red stone. "It's a class ring," he said flatly. Then, rubbing away as much of the dirt as he could, he squinted to read VANDERBILT UNIVERSITY and the year, 1954. "You found this in the grave," he said, trying to register the significance of what he studied.

"Is it your father's?"

Davis remembered how squeamish his father had been about rings. He couldn't wear even his wedding band. Claustrophobia overwhelmed him, a certainty that he could never get it off. It had been a point of tension in the family, because his mother thought a ring was an extension of the wedding vows. "People will think you don't love me," she would complain. "They'll suspect you're playing around."

"Davis," Ann Louise said softly, calling him back to the moment.

"Uh, no. No, it's not my father's. He didn't wear rings. Anyway, he never went to college." Davis was tipping the ring, trying to find an inscription or initials inside the band.

"I don't think there's anything engraved, but I'll take a closer look in better light." Her hand entered the flashlight beam, and Davis placed the ring in her small, cupped palm. "Come on, let's get out of here."

As she stood waiting for him to get up, Davis asked if the ring might have come off the finger of the hand and arm he had found. "Or could it have been dropped by a gravedigger?"

"How many Vandy grads in their mid-sixties do you think are digging graves for a living?"

"Well, it's not my father's. So how do we explain it?"

"*We* don't explain anything. I'll drop you at your mother's place and call tomorrow about what I find out."

Davis got to his feet prepared to protest, but Ann Louise had moved away already. He swung the flashlight beam in an arc ahead of him as he walked in the direction of the car. She was nowhere to be seen. He wasn't afraid to be in the cemetery at night, but this vanishing act unsettled him. Unless she jogged back to the car, she should be only a few steps ahead; but when he stopped to listen for the swish of her nylon running suit, he heard nothing.

When he didn't find her at the car, he began calling her name in the forlorn, urgent way a child calls for a lost pet. Traffic on the street was intermittent, and Davis ducked from view each time headlights lit up the roadside. One car turned into the cemetery entrance, idled for a few moments, and then backed out, continuing in the same direction. "Kids looking for a place to park," he thought.

Suddenly, Ann Louise was next to him, on the other side of the low stone wall. "Could you have made a little more noise?" she asked sarcastically.

"Where'd you go? I thought you had fallen into an open grave."

She was fumbling with something at her side, and Davis realized she was holstering a gun. "Heard something."

"Well, what was it?"

"Just the dead shuffling in their boxes."

"You thought somebody else was out there, didn't you?"

"Look, I always err on the side of caution. I've drawn down on everything from june bugs to leaky faucets. It was probably the coons that dragged off the arm you found."

"Just being in a cemetery at night makes you jumpy?" When she didn't respond, he wondered how high she'd jump if he yelled "Boo!" Might pull her gun and start firing into the dark. Then, with mock seriousness, he said, "Guns don't work with ghosts and zombies, you know."

"Look, smart-ass, we've had lots of vandalism in the cemeteries around here. Now and then we luck out and catch a couple of kids pushing over grave markers."

Before he could stop himself, Davis was saying, "I met a guy who was working on a vandal-proof graveyard." Usually, he would have cast himself in the role. It felt strange to modify his technique. "Anyhow, he's developing some kind of photosensitive system that detects any sudden movement through a ninety-degree angle. Don't ask me how it works, but he swears it will light up a graveyard like Yankee Stadium."

Ann Louise was laughing as she got into the car and pulled far enough from the wall for Davis to get in. "Pretty good," she said as he sat down and slammed the door. "You know how I can get in touch with this guy?"

Davis felt his face grow warmer. "You think I made it up, don't you."

After a silent moment, Ann Louise started the engine.

Davis said nothing, and when the car stopped in front of his mother's house, he got out. When Ann Louise rolled down her window and said she would call him, he raised a hand in acknowledgment but didn't look back.

Inside the house, Davis felt his mother's absence, a palpable presence, vestigial ache of a lopped-off part of his life. She might call out at any moment, asking where he'd been. The expectation was so strong that at first Davis simply glanced at the purse dropped on the chair nearest the door, just where his mother always left it as she stepped out of her shoes. He half expected to see her shoes, black flats side by side, so evenly squared that to step into them would be to stand at attention.

Lifting the purse by the straps, carefully, like a bag with a copperhead coiled inside, Davis held it at arm's length. Black. Big enough to contain a bowling ball and almost that heavy. It hadn't just dropped from the vapor. Someone had a key and might still be in the house. Moving quietly from room to room, Davis took shallow breaths and braced himself for the jolt that didn't come. He was alone.

At the dining room table he unzipped the main compartment and dumped the contents: lipstick, a large bottle of Anacin, a ring of keys, crumpled tissues, pepper spray, another romance novel, a worn wallet with attached coin purse, a pack of cigarettes, and a strip of three condoms. He moved the items around like checkers on a game board, touching the condoms, thinking, "No, not my mother." And the cigarettes. She had kicked the habit years ago. There wasn't an ashtray anywhere, and Davis would know if anyone regularly smoked in the house. The bitter scent would be woven into the carpeting and the curtains.

Moving his hand around inside like a conjurer who might extract a rabbit next, he found three linty breath mints. In the zippered side pockets, several gasoline-card receipts and some expired fast-food coupons. An accordion of foggy plastic windows unfolded when he opened the wallet: a driver's license, voter registration card, a picture of Davis's father, and one of Davis taken at least ten years ago. The money pocket held eight dollars, all ones. Unsnapping the coin pouch, he spilled everything onto the table. In the little pile of dimes and quarters was a tightly folded piece of paper, smaller than a nickel. When he opened it, Davis read "Block D, 1322 Perimeter Road." He held the purse upside down and shook it hard. A penny and two more dimes clattered out.

The purse lay deflated, a punctured lung, and Davis likewise felt the energy drain out of him as he looked down at the important items of his mother's daily life. But something was missing. The pills. His mother had often said, "I take so many I rattle," and she carried them with her everywhere. If some things had been taken out of the purse, then others could have been added; and Davis wondered who had invented this image of his mother.

Stupid thought. The pills were probably removed at the hospital by doctors trying to determine what medications she used. These were his mother's effects. The cigarettes, the condoms, the dumb-ass romance novel. This was Ellen Banks. Sweet little Ellen, the stoic widow.

But who had returned the purse? Who had a key to the house? Davis was breathing rapidly, too rapidly. He needed to invent a story, a Ben Blau diversion; but nothing came to him, and he lifted the empty purse to his face and breathed deeply. Familiar smell of leather. Strange smell.

CHAPTER 7

DAVIS WAS TRYING to decide if it was too late to call Ann Louise when the phone clattered. Half a ring and he answered.

"Good, you're still up. Come on down to the station and I'll show you something guaranteed to keep you awake the rest of the night."

Davis said, "Ten minutes," then thought hard after hanging up. She did say she was at the station. Wishful thinking on his part that she might be at home, that her offer was a proposition of a more personal kind. "The station," he repeated to himself mechanically, wondering if it was still on Commerce Street.

There were so few cars out at two A.M. that Davis felt himself transported back to the little town of his childhood. He might be a child, dreaming himself old enough to drive, motor idling at empty intersections when the lights went red. What was it he wanted to do? Where was he going? In the dream, the driving was aimless. Streets uncoiled past darkened houses; and through his rolled-down windows, he felt the place around him, a pressure equalized. This was his destination.

He drove past the police department and parked uphill in a large lot where the old Hotel Montgomery once stood, torn down so long ago he barely remembered it; he might not have remembered it at all if he and his parents hadn't stood across from the building each year to watch the Christmas parade. Even then it had been a hulking backdrop, empty and dangerous, crumbling in on itself.

Too many memories. Davis shut them down by pricking his finger to take a blood sugar reading in the glow of the dash-lights. This was the here and now—340. He prepared the syringe for the insulin he needed. Santa went past in a candy-cane coach, the last float. Voices of the crowd dispersing became two policemen, off-duty and headed home. Davis concealed his needle and got out of the car.

Ann Louise was waiting just inside the front door and held it open as Davis came up the steps. She led him through more doorways, past a little room lit with computer screens and the blinking buttons of phones. "911," she said. When they reached her cubicle at the far end of a room laid out like a maze of hedges, she motioned to a straight-back chair and sat down in the swiveler behind her desk. Davis stood a moment, looking at the carpeted walls of her small space, then eased himself onto the hard vinyl seat.

"What kind of shift do you work?" he asked.

"Depends on what I'm investigating. Hours don't mean much when you've got a case going."

"Do you have a case?"

"You tell me," she countered, handing him a yearbook. It was from Vanderbilt University, 1954. "Look up Winningham in the graduating class."

"Where'd you get the piece of history?" he asked, holding the corner near his nose, inhaling the musky past.

Ann Louise winked. "Nashville's only a forty-five-minute drive from here. Less if you turn on the lights and siren."

Davis flipped the pages, pausing now and then at a face smiling out at him in black and white. "Charles Winningham?" he asked finally, index finger rubbing the crew cut as if he could feel the bristle.

"Now look at this." Ann Louise handed over a thick folder, and Davis fumbled it atop the yearbook, which he kept open on his lap. Inside were forms and newspaper clippings. The headline on top of the pile read PROMINENT CLARKSVILLE AT-TORNEY STILL MISSING. Davis fingered through the articles beneath words like "mystery" and "vanished" and "foul play."

"We never found him."

Davis was having trouble connecting the yearbook and the case file. Even when Ann Louise said, "The ring," he still couldn't make sense of it.

"Charles Winningham disappeared eight years ago," she told him. "Some said he ran off with a secret lover; some said he was murdered. Made quite a splash around here, as you can see. The question now is, who's buried in your daddy's grave?"

Davis was reading an interview typescript. "Pardon?" he said, looking up distractedly.

"If the ring we found came from the arm you say you pulled through the wall of your daddy's grave, either he was wearing Winningham's ring or that was Charles Winningham's hand and arm."

Davis closed the folder and sat speechless. Finally, he asked, "Why does the ring have to belong to Winningham? Did you find an inscription inside the band?"

"No name or initials. But we found it in a grave that was open at exactly the time old Chuck, a 1954 Vandy grad, dropped out of sight forever."

"What if it's just some freak coincidence? We found a ring somebody else lost years ago."

"Could be, but I think we've got cause to exhume your father."

Davis jumped to his feet. "I came home to bury my mother, not dig up my father. Let's leave the dead alone."

"Aren't you the guy who wanted to dig up his father and sue the undertaker for selling him a shoddy coffin? I can get a court order without your consent, but it would be a lot easier if you'd help out. Either way, we're going to have a look in your daddy's grave." Her voice had become emotionless, official.

Davis walked out of the cubicle and wound among the partitions. Then he wheeled and shouted, "Look, if my father isn't in his grave, where the hell is he? You're trying to trade one lost man for another."

"I'm trying to do my job," she said flatly, looking at him over the top of her carpeted wall.

"How soon would the exhumation take place?"

"By tomorrow afternoon." Then, looking at her watch and realizing midnight had passed, she revised herself. "This afternoon. If you'll sign the consent form, we can have everything done before dark."

Davis hesitated, then signed the paper she placed in front of him, her fingertip resting just above the line.

"I'll fill in everything else and see the judge as soon as his office opens this morning. Go home and get some sleep. I'll call you when I know anything."

"Does Winningham have family living here?"

"I think his wife's still in Clarksville. Why?"

"Let's show her the ring before you go to court."

Ann Louise seemed about to balk, but then said, "I'll pick you up at seven-thirty."

●

The doorbell rang at seven-fifteen. Davis had tried to stay up all night but fell asleep in his mother's recliner, her empty purse in his lap. Clearing his throat was an amphibian adjustment, out of the pond of sleep onto the slippery bank of another day. His father had called this "the systems check"—eyes blurry, neck a little stiff, tongue a foreign object. When he finally tottered to the door and opened it, Ann Louise laughed and said, "Good morning, sunshine."

"God, how I hate cheerful morning people," he said, unsteady on his feet, rubbing his eyes.

"Cheerful people will probably return the favor. You don't look so good. More diabetes problems?"

"More like sleep deprivation. Why'd we have to start so early?"

"I thought you wanted to meet Marie Winningham, and I was hoping to catch her before her first cup of coffee. People are more honest when they're not completely awake."

Concentrating on taking a blood sugar sample, Davis was having trouble pricking his finger. When he clicked the lancet device a third time, the point went deep enough to make him wince. Seeing Ann Louise grimace, he said, "We'll do yours next." She didn't respond but leaned over to read the meter when the figure appeared—117. "First normal reading I've had since I got here," Davis said, immediately feeling better.

"You've got time for a quick shower," Ann Louise offered, seating herself in the recliner.

When Davis emerged from the bathroom, Ann Louise was sitting in the same place but had clearly done some wandering. "What's all that stuff on the dining room table?"

"Been investigating, have you?"

"Hey, I'm a cop. What can you expect?"

"Those are the contents of my mother's purse."

"Geez, I'd hate to think somebody would dump my purse and take inventory. Might as well do a brain probe."

"Yeah? I'll bet you don't have a strip of condoms in your bag."

"That information is given out on a need-to-know basis."

Was she flirting? Maybe he should press the moment to see what would happen. A great follow-up line, that's what he needed—something like "My credentials give me full access." No, no, too aggressive. A teaser would be better. Shit! How could he be so awkward with a woman? Might as well be seventeen. There she was, waiting for his comeback. The moment was pure potential. Anything could happen. Or nothing. Either way, the kinetic energy would dissipate, was dissipating. Then she was standing, moving toward the door.

"Are you coming?"

God, what a question! Maybe he should touch her shoulder, turn her around, make some kind of cinematic move. She had to know what he was thinking. He couldn't take his eyes off the back of her neck, couldn't think of anything to say except her name. When she turned and looked at him, he still didn't have a follow-up line.

"What?" She sounded puzzled and impatient. And when he said nothing, she asked again, this time lifting her hands and letting them fall in a gesture of exasperation. She didn't get it. Or he didn't. Either way, nothing was going to happen.

•

The Winningham house was in an older section of town, one of the original gentry zones. Davis could remember driving by it as a teenager cruising the town with time to fill. It had impressed him then, but now looked like fake Frank Lloyd Wright, a single-level brick built to follow the contour of a small ridge. The main door was in the exact center of the broken crescent design. "Predictable," thought Davis. But the hand-lettered sign tacked to the door was not: CHEMICAL-FREE ZONE. WARNING! IF YOU HAVE HAD A CHEMICAL EXPOSURE IN THE PAST 48 HOURS, DO NOT ENTER.

"I guess no one from the plutonium lab is welcome," Davis observed, wondering silently if the drain cleaner he had poured into the toilet at his mother's house less than two days ago constituted an exposure.

When Ann Louise rang the bell, a woman's face appeared in one of the long glass panels beside the door. Another minute and the door opened hesitantly, the same face now partly hidden by a dust mask covering the mouth and nose, a white elastic band biting into each ear. The woman kept her eyes fixed on them as she left the door open and backed away as if they were stalking her. She was a tall woman, big-boned and well filled out, hair chopped off short. She wore faded khaki, like a uniform, rumpled and stripped of insignia.

"Mrs. Winningham?" Ann Louise asked tentatively. "Mrs. Winningham, I'm from the Clarksville Police Department." She extended her identification, which the woman waved off.

They were now in a bare room with a freestanding stone fireplace in the center. It was meant to be the showpiece of the house but seemed misplaced in a room stripped down to unvarnished floors and walls scrubbed back to the original plaster. Looking from side to side, Davis saw that there was no place to sit. No furniture of any kind. No curtains. No pillows. No rugs. He had seen more hospitable campsites.

Mrs. Winningham had rounded the fireplace partly and stopped. Ann Louise and Davis stopped, too, twenty feet away and blocked from her by stone and mortar.

"Don't come any closer." The voice was stronger than Davis expected, even muffled by the mask. "Fumes of any kind might kill me—dye in clothing, shampoo scent in someone's hair." She waited, apparently to let this information seep in, and Davis kept thinking she looked too strapping to be susceptible to anything short of a dose of rat poison.

"Mrs. Winningham, I have to ask you something," Ann Louise began, but before she could continue, the woman began to gasp and back away.

"You're wearing perfume, aren't you. You'll have to leave immediately." She was making a sweeping motion with the back of her right hand while firmly holding her mask with the left.

"It's about your husband, Mrs. Winningham." Ann Louise ignored the woman's forced dry cough, which rang like hatchet blows in the empty room. Ann Louise's voice echoed faintly in the hollow space, "Your husband."

Mrs. Winningham stopped sweeping them out but backed farther away and waited.

"Can you identify this ring for us?" Ann Louise started toward her but then placed the ring on the edge of the fireplace between them.

Mrs. Winningham looked at it without moving. "I'll have to get the people in to purify this room," she said in a near monotone. Then she screamed, "Get out! Get out! Charlie took his rings when he left."

Davis stepped forward and pocketed the ring, then turned with Ann Louise and left the house. He expected to hear the door slamming behind them, but it remained open, and Marie Winningham's hatcheting resonated within.

Once they were inside the car, Ann Louise placed both hands on the steering wheel and said, "Well, that was different."

Davis felt like laughing, but nothing more than a small "huh" came out. Marie Winningham made Ben Blau look like a bad amateur. He was certain that, somewhere in the house, she closeted herself with whiskey and cigarettes, spraying the air with pine freshener. "A wasted trip," he said as Ann Louise started the engine.

Looking over her left shoulder and backing out, Ann Louise said, "Doesn't matter. I put someone on the court order for the exhumation before I left the station."

Davis felt a flash of anger. His request to postpone the hearing until they had seen Marie Winningham had not been honored. "What if she had said it definitely wasn't her husband's ring?" he asked, trying not to sound as pissed off as he felt.

"Well, she didn't. Besides, it's somebody's, and my money's still on Charles Winningham. Don't you need some breakfast?"

Davis let his silence stand for assent and tried to guess where they were headed. When Ann Louise turned in to the crowded parking lot at Moss's Café, he said, "You've gotta be kidding. I thought this place went under years ago."

"Some parts of the old town just won't die. Peel away all the franchises and the people who came here looking for a New South and it's the same old place you and I grew up in."

Even when Davis was a kid, Moss's was an anachronism, a cramped roadside diner attached to a gas station on what was then the edge of town. The B. F. Goodrich plant had been right across the highway, and the café's main business came from the rubber workers. McDonald's had already stunned the town with its OVER ONE MILLION SERVED sign, and the death of originals like this greasy eatery was assured. Still, here was Moss's, looking exactly the way Davis remembered it—a short counter facing the kitchen, half a dozen Formica-topped tables with chairs jumbled around them, the sound of frying, food steam in the air.

Seeing them come in, a man at the counter moved down one stool to make room for Ann Louise and Davis to sit side by side. "What'll it be, darlin'?" a huge woman in splattered white was asking Ann Louise before she was seated.

"Regular breakfast. Scramble the eggs."

Realizing the woman was looking at him, Davis said, "The same. And coffee."

"Coffee comes with it," Ann Louise whispered, and Davis suddenly felt conspicuous. "So do grits."

"I don't like grits," Davis protested, swiveling on his seat to have a look around.

The clientele was a strange cross-section: mostly men, some in suits, others in coveralls or jeans. Everyone talked at once, and whenever a table opened up, more people plopped into the chairs and began loud conversations.

"This time tomorrow, they'll be talking about Charles Winningham," Ann Louise remarked, reading his mind.

"You're bound to go through with this business, then."

"I told you. I'm a cop. It's what I do."

"And what if you dig up nobody but my poor father, who's been at peace for the past eight years?"

"I'll apologize."

Their orders appeared simultaneously, two chipped oval platters with eggs, sausage patties, and grits oozing butter. Two big biscuits teetered on the edge. Davis had no insulin with him but needed to eat. He promised himself he would balance everything out later with an injection.

"Hey, hey," someone called behind them. "If it isn't Lieutenant Wilson. Cuff me, sweetie. If I didn't do it, I'd sure like to."

Davis was turning around when Ann Louise put her hand on his arm and said, "Let it pass. Like I said, it's the same old town."

"Get on outta here, Marvin," called an enormous man from behind the counter. "Unless you want me to kick your ass this early in the day."

As he pushed through the door, Marvin made a sound— "Umm-um!"—that brought the big man forward in a mock charge.

"Sorry, Ann Louise. Breakfast's on me today."

"Don't worry about it, Jerry. Let me introduce you to Davis Banks."

Jerry stuck out a loin-sized hand and said, "Banks, Banks, where do I know that name from?"

"It's just one of those names, like Rivers or Fields," Davis said, pulling his hand back over the counter.

"Who's your daddy?"

"Ralph Banks."

Jerry was still coming up blank, but he persisted. "What's he do?"

"He was in the insurance business. Worked for Life of Georgia for thirty years," Davis lied.

"That must be it, then. Musta met him when he was in here selling insurance."

Davis agreed, "Probably."

While Jerry was trying to connect with the Banks family, Ann Louise's cell phone had chirped inside her purse, and she had engaged in a short, mumbled conversation, of which Davis could make out nothing. Now she turned to him and said, "Everything's set for two o'clock this afternoon. You want to be there, don't you?" The question indicated that she expected

him to say yes. "I've got a bunch of stuff to take care of between now and then, so let me drop you off at your mother's.
You've probably got things you need to do. Right?" she asked.

Davis couldn't think of a single thing. Then he glanced
down at the smeared plate in front of him and remembered his
insulin. "Right," he responded.

Jerry turned from a table he was clearing and pushed the
door open for them. Davis had to shuffle sideways past Jerry's
large stomach, and he paused a moment to say, "Next time
we'll talk life insurance." Jerry's smile weakened a little at the
corners.

CHAPTER 8

Davis watched Ann Louise drive away, then stood looking at his mother's house. He didn't want to go inside but needed his blood meter and insulin.

The contents of his mother's purse were just as he had left them on the table, and as he passed by on his way to the bathroom, he picked up the condoms and the cigarettes and dropped them into the kitchen trash can. Looking back, he considered how easy it was to edit a life. Ellen now looked more like his version of her—his mother.

No point in checking blood sugar to find out the obvious. So he drew the amount he needed for the breakfast at Moss's into the syringe, thumping the needle to clear the air bubbles. Then he squirted the contents onto the palm of his hand. Such a small amount. A smell like musky Vaseline. How could the absence of so little insulin mean the difference between life and death? "The elixir of life," he mused, then filled the syringe again, this time to its limit, and held it up to the light. "Or maybe death." Lifting his shirttail once more, Davis touched the tip of the needle to his skin. No sensation. He had taken injections for so long he couldn't feel the point. But there was power in this moment, the power to overdose on the only thing that would keep him alive. He felt the irony as a shortness of breath, a chill at the nape of the neck. Until a bead of blood formed where the needle slightly depressed the skin, Davis couldn't break his focus. It was his blood, his life. He pushed the plunger, watching the little stream arc into the sink, then drew up the right amount and jabbed himself, wanting to live.

•

Needing to escape the emptiness of the house, Davis decided to drive somewhere, anywhere. He was about to back into the street when he checked the rearview mirror and saw something behind him—LIER, in letters large enough to cover the whole back window. Black letters which, when he glanced over his shoulder, turned inside out and backward. His first thought was the need for literacy among vandals. Could start a school for young thugs, teach them to put the "n" on "damn" and the "e" on "asshole." Something in him wanted not to rub the word off the glass but to correct it. He got out and scraped at the "E" with a fingernail. Shoe polish.

"It was a kid in a green truck." The voice was disembodied, and Davis couldn't locate its source until an elderly woman in the adjoining yard stood up and stepped from behind the bush where she was digging dandelions. She leaned to read the word.

"Did he do anything besides write this on the window?"

"Don't think so. He parked up the street from my house and walked back. Looked kind of sneaky, so I stayed put and kept an eye on him. Would have called the police, but he was gone in a minute."

"It's just a little practical joke." Davis smiled. "Nothing to worry about."

"In my day, being called a liar, spelled right or not, was nothing to joke about."

The woman watched as he backed down the driveway and into the street, and he could see her straining to read the word again as he pulled away. He stopped at the first gas station, intending to scrub the window, but changed his mind. The word suited him. Why should he reject being tagged with it, especially when it also indicted anyone who drove behind him? Maybe this was something like Uncle Oscar's revelation, this being invested with the Word.

Davis hadn't realized how wounded Gaylon was. Hadn't counted on him being the vengeful type, but then he didn't really know the kid. Hell, he had just tried to show him a short-cut across some pretty rocky ground. If the boy was too proud to appreciate it, too damn bad. Maybe he'd like a big black word on his shiny truck. A couple of words. Maybe a whole goddamned sentence. But he didn't deserve it. Anyone who couldn't spell any better than that wasn't worth a visitation.

It was a little past nine. Almost five hours before he was due at the cemetery. Almost three before visitation at Berkley's, where Aunt Goldie would be managing the room like a maître d'. Time to kill. To kill time. Killing time. He turned the phrases over and around in his mind until the words lost their meaning and he began saying them aloud, tapping the steering wheel in cadence—time to kill time to kill time to kill timetokilltimetokilltime. Before he knew it, he was singing a medley of songs, "I'm Sorry," "Moon River," and "Strangers in the Night," all with three words as lyrics—time to kill. The universal language. Laughing, he challenged himself to think of a song that the words couldn't be made to fit but got only as far as "Somewhere over the Rainbow" before cracking himself up: "Time . . . tooooo . . . kill time to kill . . . time to kill." Music was dead time. Time measured and boxed and repeatedly disinterred, commemorating not only the time of its own composition or performance but also the time expended listening to it. Music was death. This thought struck him with such force that he pulled off the road and got out of the car. "Shit, I've wasted my life," he said, kicking at the gravel on the shoulder.

A utility truck pulled up behind him and one of the men in the cab yelled, "Havin' trouble?"

Davis walked back to them and said, "No, just thought I'd left my gas cap when I filled up a mile or so back, but I didn't."

"So, what's that on your rear window?" asked the other man, leaning in Davis's direction.

"That? Oh, that's a French word, 'lee-air.' Hard to translate. Means something like 'good journey.' Some friends of mine wrote it there when I took them to the airport. A little Parisian goodwill, I guess."

"Whatever you say." The driver put the truck in gear and edged back into the flow of traffic.

Lee Air might be a nineteen-fifties subdivision. Davis inhaled the exhaust of passing cars and let his mind drift with the fumes, thinking of the old billboard on the Fort Campbell Highway. BEL AIR ESTATES, it lied, with a vaguely antebellum rendition of a house. In reality, the development was a scalped field of ranch-style dwellings with attached garages. Close to the army base, it attracted young lieutenants and their families. Olive drab and squalling babies. Homes for the homeless and the far away from home. The kid from New Jersey or Michigan with a bride from the Phillipines or Clarksville, culture shock

one way or the other. Trying to make sense of the language, trying to hold down a helping of boiled okra. LIVE ON YOUR OWN
BLOCK, the billboard had exhorted.

"Block." It was a reference to an army-base address. Davis
found himself remembering the address hidden in his mother's
coin purse. What was the name of the street? His wallet—he
had put the slip of paper in his own wallet. Fanning out the
bills on the passenger seat, he found it tucked between two
twenties. Block D, 1322 Perimeter Road. Couldn't be anywhere but on the army base. It tantalized like the answer to a
question he hadn't yet formulated.

As he neared Fort Campbell and the Kentucky state line,
Davis tried to remember where the main gate was, then turned
abruptly at a sign marked VISITORS. There was the little booth
with its blockade arms, exactly as it had been in his childhood;
a soldier with MP insignias on his uniform and helmet stepped
smartly out of the booth and bent down to look through
Davis's window.

"Yes, sir?" he clicked in a brisk voice, his intonation
halfway between a question and an exclamation.

"I'm looking for this address," Davis said, holding up the
creased slip of paper.

After giving it the slightest of glances, the soldier stepped
back from the car and said, "Straight ahead, sir, then follow the
signs to Block D."

"Thank you," Davis said, hesitating a moment, wondering
if he should say "dismissed." This caricature of a guard was almost amusing. When his father had brought the family here to
visit friends in the sixties, the security had seemed much more
menacing, and the MPs had frightened Davis as they walked
around the car, asking to look inside the trunk and peering
through the windows at him and his mother. As Davis pulled
away now, he could see, in the mirror, the young soldier disap-

pear into his little booth, like a clockwork figure after the hour has struck.

Block D was easy to find, and Perimeter Road, true to its name, turned out to be the outermost street in the residential area. The buildings all looked the same—green and white duplexes with an occasional playground between. Kids at recess were throwing a football, and some of them turned to watch as Davis drove slowly past, trying to read the numbers on the houses. When he stopped and got out of the car, one of them kicked the ball hard in the opposite direction, and they all ran farther away. From the sidewalk, he could see the numbers plainly. Immediately in front of him was 1508. Next door was 1510, so he turned around and walked the opposite way, leaving the car at the curb. When he reached 1322, he stood so long looking at the number that someone came to the front door.

"Whatcha lookin' for?"

Unable to see the person who spoke from the other side of a screen, Davis tilted his head and walked toward the house, squinting for better vision. "I'm looking for an old army buddy of mine."

The door opened, and a thin woman stepped onto the front porch. "This is the Haupt residence," she said.

The woman's age was hard to determine—somewhere in her forties. Her thinness seemed unnatural, as if she were recovering from a terrible illness. "Bill Haupt?" Davis asked tentatively, hoping his dart would strike the right name.

"No, Roger," said the woman, coming all the way out to the front steps, her hands caught up in her skirt as if she were drying them. "I'm his wife." Seeming hopeful of a conversation, she said, "My name's Amy."

"I think I've got the wrong Haupt. Bill and I did a tour of 'Nam right at the end of the war. Was your husband in-country, in Vietnam, I mean?"

"Yeah, he was there. Middle name's Dale, though, so he's prob'ly not the guy you're lookin' for."

"Big fellow with sandy-blond hair. Wasn't married at the time but had a girlfriend somewhere out west, Wyoming or Utah." Davis was in total free fall now, tumbling through the descent of his own inventions.

"My husband comes home for early lunch. Should be here any time." She abruptly turned and went back into the house, leaving Davis alone.

Had he struck too close or too far from the mark? Either she was irritated to think about one of her husband's old girlfriends or suspicious of Davis's story. As he turned toward his car, a jeep pulled up beside him and a man wearing sergeant's stripes jumped out, saying to the driver, "See you at 1300."

Sizing up Davis, the sergeant snarled, "Who the hell are you?" emphasizing every word as if Davis were supposed to lip-read.

"Roger Haupt, I presume."

"Never-the-fuck mind who I am. What are you doing nosing around my house? You selling something? No salesmen are allowed on this base."

"I found your address in my mother's purse."

"I don't damn well care where you found my address; answer my question. What are you doing here?"

Davis started to walk away, but Haupt grabbed him by the arm and spun him back. "I want a goddamned answer."

"Afraid your wife will find out about my mother?" The question was a desperate counterpunch, a wild roundhouse swing that shocked even Davis. Haupt still had hold of Davis's arm and began guiding him toward the playground equipment in an adjoining field.

"What did you say to my wife?"

"That's between her and me."

"Listen, asshole, you don't know what you're doing. You don't know anything, and you're messing around where you don't belong."

Feeling the anger rise in him, Davis pulled away from Haupt's grasp and said, "Yeah, my mother was seeing a married man, who might have killed her for all I know, and it's none of my business." Rushed along by his own line of free associations, he was speaking without formulating thoughts.

"What the hell are you talking about?"

"You were with her when she died, weren't you?"

"Who told you that?"

"Well, weren't you?"

Haupt turned and sat down in one of the swings. For a few moments, he rocked back and forth, studying the sand beneath his feet, then looked up. "You're older than in any of the pictures I've seen. Why is this so damned important to you?"

"I need to know what happened to my mother."

Haupt lifted his feet, letting himself swing slightly. "Yeah, I was with her."

The confirmation of Davis's wild guess stunned him. Haupt looked absurd in a child's swing, wearing his camouflage fatigues, and Davis had a sudden vision of him as a playground bully. "Well . . . ?" he asked.

"Well, what?"

"Don't be an asshole, Sergeant. You know exactly what I mean. Details—I want the details."

Looking up with what might have been a half grin, Haupt began, "First she got pretty sick and threw up all over the place, and then . . ."

"Tell me where you and my mother were when she died." Davis felt light-headed.

"I thought you wanted the dee-tails," Haupt mocked.

"Where were you when she died?"

"Nashville, at the Howard Johnson's near downtown."

"Nashville?"

"We'd been in Printer's Alley, listening to live bands and drinking a little, and decided to check into a hotel instead of driving back to Clarksville."

"And my mother died in the frigging Howard Johnson's?"

"Not many of us get to choose where we die. Anyhow, she wasn't actually pronounced dead until she got to the hospital."

"Which one?"

"What does it matter? The heart attack was so massive no one could have done anything for her if she had been in a hospital when it happened."

"You took her back to Clarksville, didn't you?" Davis asked, the incredulity in his voice edged with anger.

Haupt pushed off with his feet, increasing the arc of his swing.

"You son of a bitch! You put my mother in the car and drove her forty miles to Clarksville when you could have called 911 and had an ambulance at Howard Johnson's in minutes."

Haupt still said nothing, the darker parts of his camouflage uniform making it seem as if chunks of him were disappearing.

"You could have saved her life."

"Look, I had her at the Memorial Hospital emergency room in thirty minutes, and she was still breathing when I got there."

"Oh, wow! My hero!" Davis said sarcastically. "I can just see you now, doing ninety on the interstate while my mother dies in the backseat."

When Haupt replied, he was so close that Davis could hear a small rasp in the man's sinuses. He hadn't seen Haupt get out of the swing. "You make trouble for me, and I'm just the man who can return the favor."

Taking a step back, Davis felt his heart quicken, and his voice tensed with false bravado. "I'm not afraid of you."

"Maybe you should be. I'm a dangerous man."

"What if I told your wife about my mother?"

"You wouldn't want to do that."

"Maybe I do. Maybe I want to repay you for taking my mother on a death drive up I-24."

"She wouldn't believe you."

"She seemed pretty suspicious already, from my short talk with her." Davis waited for a response. The kids who had been playing football had all gone back to their studies, and the schoolyard was silent.

"Okay, what do you want from me?"

"The truth."

Haupt huffed a little laugh. "Big request."

"Just tell me about you and my mother."

Drawing in a deep breath, Haupt exhaled slowly, then said, "Not much to tell, really. We met at a bar. Just hit it off, you know. She knew I was married, but it didn't make any difference to her. Neither one of us was a kid, so we understood what we were getting ourselves into."

"And you stayed over at her house?"

"Sometimes. Or we'd go to Nashville. One time we drove all the way over to Branson, in Missouri, and spent a weekend."

"Why do you suppose she never told me about any of this?"

"Why do you think? Look, I'm sorry she's dead. I cared about her, you know. We had some good times together."

"Then why did you drag her back to Clarksville instead of getting her some help?"

"She stopped me. I started to call 911, but she said she didn't want us to be caught together in Nashville. Said we could make it to Clarksville if I'd hurry."

"She said all this while she was throwing up and having a heart attack?"

"Believe what you want. You asked for the truth."

"And she was still alive when you got her to Memorial Hospital?"

"Yeah. I carried her into the emergency room and put her on a gurney myself. They were working on her when I left."

"You left her there alone?"

"I'm not proud of that, but it's what your mother wanted. She was terrified someone would find out about us."

"And you discovered her purse in your car."

"Right."

"And you returned it while I was away from the house today."

"Yes."

Davis walked away, down the street toward his car, and Sergeant Haupt stood so still that he became a blotch on the playground green.

CHAPTER 9

DAVIS MADE A sloppy U-turn, one he had to back up to complete, and looked straight ahead as he passed 1322. His hands gripped the wheel so hard his arms were shaking, and he couldn't breathe. Out of view of the Haupts', he pulled over and rolled down the window, taking in air as deeply as he could.

Sergeant Haupt didn't fit. He was the wrong man for Ellen Banks, a kind she never could like. A bulldog with cropped blond hair, tattoos on his forearms. A man wearing the signature paunch of his middle fifties. And yet they had known each other—in the biblical sense. Chastising himself for his cautious, almost prudish observation, Davis forced a thought: "My mother was fucking a goddamned GI. A married man."

But the baldness of the assertion, even made silently, caused him to shift nervously in his seat.

"Maybe it's all a lie. Maybe the story could be told another way. Whose word do I have but Haupt's? Hell, I essentially made up the story. All he did was embellish it." What if they never had an affair at all but were acquainted only through Haupt's forwardness? Maybe he was someone she met by chance and didn't really like. What if he had attached himself to her and she was trying to get rid of him?

Maybe the heart attack had occurred while she was in Haupt's company—at the mall, perhaps—and he had rushed her to the hospital, not noticing her purse on the floorboard until sometime later. And Haupt could have made his own key to the house, once he had possession of hers, on the chance that she would recover and then he would have a decided advantage over her.

The more Davis unspooled such fictions, the more real they seemed. In some respects, they were more plausible than what Haupt had told him. At least the narratives he was developing made better sense in terms of what he knew about his own mother.

"He was taking advantage of her, and now he's screwing with my head because it makes him feel powerful." But the truth had become negotiable, not fixed; Davis realized he was fashioning his own version. Nothing is certain. That old adage winked at him from within, revealing an ambiguity he had never before realized: The one absolute certainty is nothing. In his head, the statement went round and round like a mantra: Nothing is certain nothing is certain nothing is certain.

Davis felt that familiar shaft opening inside, and he began falling into himself, saying, "Oh, God, no, not now, please,

please!" He started the engine and turned on the radio, hoping the noise would break his descent. The song was one he knew, and he sang along, loudly at first and then softer as he regained control—"Smokin' cigarettes and watchin' *Captain Kangaroo,* now don't tell me I've nothin' to do." He had always despised it, but finding it on a station his mother had preset on the dial tethered him once again to the ground.

Tipping his wristwatch, Davis saw that it was only ten-fifteen. Still almost two hours before visitation at Berkley's Funeral Home. Plenty of time to stop by his mother's house and change clothes. A dark suit for the dark occasion. Forgetting he had already started the engine, Davis turned the key in the ignition, generating a loud squeal, then pressed hard enough on the gas to rattle the midday air. Across the street, a screen door opened as he stuttered away.

Davis was so distracted by the clumsy start that he took a wrong turn and found himself suddenly in a wilderness. He knew the army owned great tracts of undeveloped land straddling the Kentucky and Tennessee state line, woods and fields used for military exercises and to create a buffer zone between whatever secrets the military kept and the prying eyes of the outside world, but he had seen the land only through chain-link fencing marked with NO TRESPASSING signs. He was looking for a place to turn around when something in the mirror caught his eye, a windshield flashing sunlight.

"The MPs," he thought, wondering if they had the authority to arrest him for being in a place marked off-limits. Studying the mirror, he lost sight of the narrow road and slammed on the brakes too late to keep from galloping head-long into and then out of a shallow ditch, coming to a standstill in a field of scrub cedar. The smell of gasoline from the flooded engine made him think of insulin, an oily sweetness that made him gag. Pushing the door open into weeds almost window high, Davis swung his legs around and started to get out when he heard someone rustling nearby.

"Stay where you are." The voice was high-pitched with youth and nervousness.

Davis tried to stand so he could see who was speaking, but the tension in the voice forced him back into his seat: "Don't move!"

"I don't have time to play army games. Okay? If you're gonna shoot me, just get it over with." Again Davis tried to stand, but this time something rushed through the weeds and slammed him back into the car. At the same moment, the door on the opposite side opened and someone grabbed him under the chin and pulled him across the front seat. When he tried to move to lessen the strain on his neck, he realized his knees were being held down by whoever had knocked him backward. His throat was narrowed by the pull—it might have had a large stone lodged in it, the way his breath wheezed and thinned. The pulsing in his ears evened out into a low roar, and his whole body convulsed just as the pressure stopped.

He lay coughing, looking at the beige headliner, unable to move even though no one was holding him now. Around him voices rose and fell like birdcalls—a twitter, then an embellishment. "Rosy-breasted nuthatch," he guessed. The beige above him hung like a winter sky in evening. "Flannel," he thought, just as someone gripped him under each arm and dragged him all the way across the seat and into the field.

Davis's coughing turned spasmodic, and he rolled onto his stomach, retching and dragging for air. Against his face, the dead weeds were reedy and smelled of dusk. But lower, closer to the ground, the green was coming in. He spat several times and sat up, expecting to see a soldier with a gun pointed at him. When he tried to look over his shoulder, his neck hurt so much he had to shift his body. No one.

"Who's there?" His voice was burred and broken. Again, "Who's there?" When no one answered, he tried to stand, moving first to his knees, then putting his weight on one foot. As he rose, he lost his balance and staggered a little before steadying himself. His mother's car sat in the weeds with both front doors open. Its dull yellow hood blunted the overhead sun.

"Jesus," Davis said, turning several times to look around the field. Still wobbly, he sat down in the dead and reviving weeds, thinking, "That bastard Haupt." But he hadn't seen Haupt, hadn't seen anyone, really. He might have been attacked by aliens, for all he knew. The thought caused a laugh that set off a fit of coughing. "Had to be Haupt." Maybe the message was that he could do whatever he wanted, without explanation, even without reason. "Sergeant God," Davis said. "Sergeant God, sir!"

Inside his mother's car, Davis picked at the sticktights that speckled his trousers and leaned over to see his face in the mirror. His neck was red, and three fingertip indentations appeared just to the left of his windpipe. Davis hooked his right thumb and forefinger beneath his chin and placed his other three fingers in the spots, where they fit exactly. The mechanics of the assault intrigued him. Was it some kind of Green Beret hold or just a clumsy grab? For a long time, he studied himself, his hand coming from beyond the view of the mirror like someone else's. He lifted his fingers one at a time, then put them down again, as if playing a saxophone.

When a sudden gust whipped through the car, Davis slid across the seat to reach the handle of the opposite door. The solid slam stunned him, and he sat like a passenger waiting for the driver to arrive. This was the nowhere zone, the place from which everyone answers "Nothing" when asked "What are you thinking?" Hard to articulate the scuttle of images, mixed and random as leaves blown along a sidewalk—his mother, Haupt, Ann Louise, his half-assed job in Des Moines. If someone who knew where to go and what to do would slide in on the driver's side, Davis could close his eyes and take the ride.

When he scooted back behind the wheel and turned the key, the engine made an oblong groan, the sound of something turning very fast around an elliptical circuit—loud, then far away, then loud, finally breaking free in a straight-line roar. Slamming his door, Davis stared over the hood for a place to steer through the field, hoping to drive out the same way he had come in, but brush raked the undercarriage, and the land was so uneven that he veered off and felt for smoother ground. He was concentrating so intently on pitch and roll that he intersected the road by accident. A charge of the engine, a final gallop, and he was once more on pavement, tires shrilling as he grappled the wheel to straighten up. When he was squarely in his lane, he placed the car in neutral and raced the engine, the way he had done at stoplights when he was a kid, then shifted back into drive and held the accelerator pedal to the floor. At first, no movement, just a steady boil of smoke at the rear; then a screeching thrust pinned Davis so hard against his seat he caught his breath.

He was still driving fast when he crossed Perimeter Road. Seeing the sign made his foot come down suddenly on the brake, and the car yawed hard, its rear end wailing forward to the right, forcing half a spin before everything came to a full stop. The engine was loping, half dying, then catching again. The smell of rubber was sickening, an industrial stench. Davis wanted to drive on but couldn't lift his foot off the brake pedal for fear the spin would continue. As long as he sat perfectly still, nothing would happen. Nothing was happening. Even death couldn't be safer. Maybe he was dead. Maybe he had been killed in the field. As a test, he took his foot from the brake. Nothing, until he eased down on the gas and turned onto Perimeter.

Not knowing what he would do when he got there, Davis drove back to Haupt's house, trying to spot numbers on the identical buildings as he trolled along. The playground and the swing set where Haupt had sat marked the place. Davis idled at the curb, leaning across the seat to stare at the front door. The screen and the shadow from the small porch roof made it impossible to tell if the door was closed. Davis thought of getting out or sounding the horn but did neither. He sat for a long time, but no one came.

"He's in there, and he knows I'm out here." Davis imagined himself in the middle of a standoff. "Wants me to make the first move so he can call the MPs. Stupid bastard." Feeling oddly triumphant, Davis lifted his middle finger as a farewell salute and slowly drove away, nosing through a maze of streets until he finally found the visitors' gate.

The guard came out of his clockwork box and signaled Davis through. But just as the blockade arm came up and the car rolled forward, the toy soldier began to yell and wave his arms. Before Davis could pull onto the highway, the guard was in front of him with both hands on the hood.

When he was certain Davis understood he was to stay put, the young man said, "Just a minute, sir," and walked to the rear of the car. For a moment, he was out of view, and Davis felt the car lift a little on its springs and heard something rasping against metal.

"Don't want to drag this down the highway," he said, holding out a tangle of brush and small limbs for Davis to see.

"Shit. So that's what's been making that racket. You know, I must have snagged that stuff when I was out in the country this morning."

The soldier looked hard at Davis. "Probably so, sir. Glad I caught sight of it before you pulled off."

Davis said, "Thanks, soldier," and, before he could stop himself, actually gave the young man a military salute as he eased into traffic. "Could be in the reserves, for all he knows. Captain . . . no, Colonel Banks." Davis felt in charge again as he gained speed along the Fort Campbell Highway.

When he looked at his watch, he saw that the crystal was broken. The second hand was still sweeping the dial, but the time couldn't be right—almost twelve-thirty—unless he had lain unconscious in the weeds for two hours. If that was the right time, he would make it to Berkley's with only a few minutes left in the visitation hour. He stared at the watch again, wondering if it had cracked when he ran off the road or if his attackers had fractured it. "Watches and clocks are supposed to stop at the exact moment of the crime or accident," Davis mused, feeling cheated. Pulling back his sleeve, he slammed his wrist into the side window. The car veered to the left with the motion, causing someone in the adjacent lane to blow his horn. "Yeah, yeah," Davis said into the windshield. The driver leered as he ripped by, but Davis looked instead at his watch. It was no longer running.

When he got to Berkley's, only a few cars speckled the parking lot, and Davis studied his watch, shattered at its last correct time. Leaning against the fender of a car near the building was Uncle Oscar, part of a circle of men, some of them smoking, occasionally spitting back onto the grass. "Nice you could make it," he drawled as Davis approached. "You been runnin' with the hound dogs, son?" A muffled laugh rippled through the group. Looking down at his clothes, Davis saw for the first time how filthy he was. Sticktights clung everywhere, and he was stained with new grass and soft earth. Stopping for a moment to consider his condition, he looked directly at

Oscar but said nothing. As he entered the building, he thought, "All the mangy dogs seem to be here," and considered stepping back outside with the remark, but he had lost the moment.

Inside, he was met by Mr. Berkley, his eyes downcast in a display of deference and respect. "Welcome, welcome," he said, finally glancing up to see Davis's face, then taking in his full presentation. "You all right, Mr. Banks?"

"Had a little accident, but no real harm done." Davis found it hard not to confront Berkley with accusations about his father's shoddy burial. "Cheap little bastard," he thought.

"There's a bathroom in my office. You're welcome to clean up a little."

Davis shook his head and continued along the corridor that materialized as his eyes adjusted to the dimness. When he reached the door leading to his mother's body, he paused to look at the guest book spread open on a small table and was offered a pen by an overly made-up young woman in a short black dress. From behind him, Mr. Berkley said, "He's a member of the immediate family, Daneen." Embarrassed, she withdrew the pen. Davis saw that the top of her dress was a fine mesh, beneath which the straps of a black slip or bra were visible. "My youngest," Mr. Berkley proudly announced. "Learning the business."

Daneen was not just Berkley's child but also his vision, an angel of the dead in a trampy dress. Pale with the same cosmetics used on the corpses, she was ghoulish but alluring.

Aunt Goldie padded up, giving Daneen a brief look of disapproval. "Thank the Good Lord, you're finally here," she said to Davis. "Everyone's been askin' 'bout you." She kept score in these matters, giving herself extra points for being the first to arrive and the last to leave. He had been assessed heavy demerits.

"Had a little trouble with the car."

Ignoring his remark and oblivious to the condition of his clothes, she continued, "The family is s'posed to be here to greet the visitors." She looked expectantly around the room, making precise little smiles and nodding at the late arrivals.

At the far end of the room, stands of gladiolas flanked the casket. No one was near his mother, whom Davis half expected to see rise from her box like the magician's assistant, showing that the saw hadn't touched her. He walked briskly to a small group hovering near the back of the room.

"Hello, hello! How good to greet you. I'm Davis Banks. Come this way and I'll introduce you to my mother. You'll have to forgive her for not getting up."

Someone's throat made a noise, midway between a choke and a chuckle, but no one moved. Even Davis stood motionless until his aunt said, "We're all under an awful stress."

"Yes, an awful stress. Heaven knows how we carry on, but we do, don't we, Aunt Goldie?" Davis stressed the words "carry on." When she began to cry, he proclaimed, "I rest my case."

He walked to the casket and, without looking at his mother, closed the lid. Then he turned to face the nearly empty room. "That's it for now, folks. Show's over." As the impresario of the dead, he took a deep bow. "That's it. Get out." His aunt had plopped onto one of the folding chairs and begun to sob, bobbing with spasms that rose into her throat at regular intervals. When she and Davis were the only ones left in the room with the corpse of Ellen Banks, Davis made a small patter of applause. "Well played, Auntie. Good show."

By the time Davis reached the front door, word of his behavior had spread into the corridor and spilled outside. Rushing in, Oscar grabbed his arm. "What the hell's goin' on?" Davis wrenched free and barked, then bayed like a hound in the musky night and pushed through the door to the parking lot. Someone said his name, but he didn't look to see who it was. Again the voice called out, a woman's. He turned long enough to see Linda standing on the sidewalk in front of the funeral home. The look on her face rushed him back to days of their marriage, one of them always leaving in the other's baleful glare. "The living dead," he thought, and as he swung the car out of the lot he howled, the sound covered by the rumble of the exhaust.

CHAPTER 10

When he got home, Davis shucked his pants, turning them inside out to keep the sticktights off the carpet, and went into the bedroom to find clean clothes. He studied his broken watch as he took it off. "Twelve twenty-eight forever," he exulted, catching sight of his face in the dresser mirror. The finger-marks on his neck had become a blotch. "You're losing your goddamned mind," said the face looking back at him. "Hey, we're under a lot of pressure, here," Davis replied, trying first for a Marlon Brando imitation and then for Jimmy Stewart. "Shit, I do need to get a grip," this time in his own weary voice.

The doorbell rang its bing-bong Hollywood tones. Wearing only his dress shirt and underwear, he swung the door open, expecting to see Ann Louise. There was Linda, doleful enough to be his widow rather than his ex-wife. Making a mock gesture of covering his privates, he said, "Just a minute," and returned wearing his inside-out pants, unzipped because the fly was backward.

"I don't think I should come in," she said.

Without replying, Davis stepped onto the small front porch. They hadn't been this close in years, and he concealed his unease with brashness. "Have a seat," he offered, plopping down and patting the step beside him.

Linda hovered over him for a moment, then descended the steps and stood in the front yard, facing him. "You all right?"

"Was I ever?"

She lifted her arms, letting them fall to her sides. "Same old Davis. Never a straight answer. Never anything the easy way."

"When did you start coloring your hair?"

"When did you start wearing your pants inside out? Anyhow, who says it's colored?"

"Well, I don't recall it being quite that dark."

"Then again, you don't recall much of anything, do you?"

"You'd be amazed at what I remember."

In the hesitation that followed, Davis thought of the days before everything went wrong, those weekend afternoons of idleness when they made room for each other and blocked out everything else. He wondered if Linda was recalling the same times, but then she said, "For example?"

"Remember that time I dropped a bowl of mashed potatoes?"

"No."

"Sure you do. You must. Right after we were married. I was showing off, mixing up a big bowl of mashed potatoes by hand instead of using the electric mixer. My arm gave out, and I dropped the whole thing. What amazed me was how far those potatoes went. Splatters everywhere. Kept turning up for weeks. I wouldn't be surprised if we could find some right now around the rungs of the chairs or up under the kitchen table."

"Don't have that dinette set anymore."

"But you remember, don't you?"

"Lots of things got dropped or broken while we were married."

"You had potatoes even on your shoes."

"Okay, so you dropped the mashed potatoes. What's the point?"

"The point is, I remember."

"So does that mean you win?" Her voice was testy.

Davis stood up, holding his fly together with his left hand and extending his right. "Thanks for checking on me. I'm okay, really. Good to see you."

Linda took his hand for a second. "I'm sorry about your mama." Then she was gone.

Back inside the house, Davis sat scratching the spots where the stickers irritated his legs. Nothing had changed between him and Linda. Irreconcilable differences. Still, he felt a rush of power at having given her a memory. The mashed-potato fiasco had never happened, but now that Linda had accepted it, she would carry it with her as one of the events of their marriage. Davis imagined her in her dotage, recounting the tale to anyone who would listen. It might even take on symbolic value for her: "Yep, I shoulda known right then that things weren't gonna last."

Altering reality by inventing a piece of the past. Amazingly simple. But while it exhilarated him, it also made him feel hollow, as if his own life were only drapery arranged by whim and misapprehension. He half believed the potato story himself.

Was this what the original Word was all about, the word that was in the beginning, first utterance of a story being made up as we go along? In the beginning was the smashed bowl of mashed potatoes.

Tugging at his pants, Davis chided himself, "Things can't be half that complicated. Or half that simple."

In the shower, he bowed his head into the rush of water and tried to stop thinking. But thinking about stopping thought was thinking. "I think too fucking much!" he burbled. The water spinning around the drain was a vanishing clock, and Davis wondered why Ann Louise hadn't stopped by on her way to the cemetery. It had to be well past two P.M.

•

By the time he got to Greenwood, the backhoe had scooped a large pile of dirt and was biting deeper into his father's grave. Crossing among the markers, he fixed on the roar of the machine, which grew louder, more serious, when it was digging. A hungry rumble. Ravenous.

An officer in uniform talking to a man dressed in surgical scrubs started toward Davis, waving him away. "Sorry, sir. This part of the cemetery is off-limits."

"I'm looking for Detective Wilson."

"And you are?"

"I'm the son of the man you're digging up."

Embarrassed, the officer turned aside and pointed toward the backhoe. "She's over there."

At that moment, Ann Louise stood up from where she had been crouching to watch the progress of the digging. She motioned to Davis and shouted, "You're late," above the roar of the digger.

Davis nodded in agreement but didn't say anything. The

hole transfixed him. At any moment, he expected to see bones or fabric. The resurrection. Gabriel's trumpet was yellow and made an awful noise. Ann Louise hovered like the angel of the afterlife, studying the deepening trough. When she stood suddenly and waved both arms, she might have been preparing to fly. The machine backed away, and the noise stopped. From somewhere near the treeline at the edge of the cemetery, two men dressed in coveralls rose and walked toward the grave. When one of them jumped in, Davis felt faint, as if he had just witnessed a suicide leap. But a voice came back from the ragged opening—"Yeah, this is about right"—and then the second man jumped in too.

"Want some coffee?" Ann Louise asked. "This is gonna take a while."

Davis followed her to a car parked on the narrow road that twisted through the cemetery.

"Sorry you weren't here when we started. Coroner's a stickler for details. Wouldn't let us wait past two. That's him in the surgical outfit." She gestured with a thermos, poured a cupful, and handed it to Davis. "We're close to the coffin, so the rest of the digging has to be done by hand. Those guys in the grave will rig up a pulley. Nothing to see, really, until they get the coffin up."

Ann Louise had turned and was sitting on the end of the front seat, her legs extending outside the car and crossed at the ankles. "I didn't know you knew Buford," she said between sips of coffee.

Davis stood leaning against the car, absently spinning his coffee inside the cup. "Knew who?"

"Buford, my ex. He said to tell you the pleasure was all his, whatever that means."

Davis felt he had come in on the middle of a conversation

without all the facts. "You're talking about your ex-husband. Right?"

"Hey, you're not having some kind of diabetic reaction, are you?"

He hadn't thought about food or insulin since that morning, and the question made him run a quick internal-systems check: none of the jittery disorientation of low blood sugar, no fatigue associated with extreme highs. "I think I'm all right, but I don't know who Buford is."

"Well, he seems to know you. Acted like you were old friends when I ran into him on my lunch break."

"Shit! It wasn't Haupt!" Davis thought. "It was Buford!" He clenched his fists and turned in a full circle, repeating the name.

"What's going on?" Ann Louise drew up her legs and tipped forward on the edge of the seat, ready to get out of the car.

Davis remembered the field, the hand compressing his throat. "That's why he didn't say anything. He wanted you to deliver the message. Jesus H. Christ!"

"Look, if you don't start making sense, I'm gonna have Donnie put you in the squad car and run you out to the emergency room."

"How long have you been divorced?"

Ann Louise gave him a critical appraisal but didn't answer.

"Is Buford the jealous type?"

A change swept Ann Louise's face as she stood and looked past Davis. "The son of a bitch is still watching me."

Remembering Ann Louise's sparsely furnished house, Davis recognized it for what it was, temporary shelter, a way station on the escape route from Buford. "The divorce wasn't his idea, I take it."

Ann Louise turned abruptly and faced Davis. "Are you gonna tell me what Buford did, or do I have to guess?"

"Let's just say he introduced himself in an unusual way."

"Buford's style would be to sneak up behind you and hit you with a brick."

Davis was surprised to find himself laughing. "That's pretty close."

"If you want to press charges, I'll bring the bastard in myself."

Ann Louise seemed disappointed when Davis said he couldn't identify him as his attacker. "Anyhow, there were two of them."

"Well, that's definitely Buford's style. Gets one of his drinking buddies to help him mug somebody."

"What's his motive?" The question was falsely naive, but Ann Louise answered it straightforwardly.

"He probably thinks you and I are fooling around."

"Does double jeopardy work in situations like this? I mean, if you're held accountable for something you didn't do, are you then free to do it?" The question sounded hopelessly complex and was too much of a come-on if Ann Louise understood it the way it was meant. Davis felt stupid and clumsy.

Distracted by her own line of thought, Ann Louise mused, "He must have been following me when I met you at the mall. When does the man work, for God's sake?"

Glad for an exit from his own forwardness, Davis asked questions about Buford's violence.

"He pushed me once or twice. Mostly, he just yelled and threw things. Didn't like my late hours on patrol and hated every man I was teamed with. Basically, he's a coward."

"Doesn't mean he isn't dangerous, just the same."

Ann Louise appeared to be weighing that statement against

her experiences with Buford when someone called her name from the grave site.

The coffin was in midair, swinging gently from the tripod pulley, and from a distance seemed to be hovering. As they drew nearer, Davis watched it sway to one side of the hole, scattering clotted earth, an old wound reopened. The workmen grappled the box like cargo from a ship's hold.

Ann Louise spoke to the coroner, who stood on the opposite side of the grave. "What do you want to do now?"

The coroner leaned to look into the hole, studied a moment, then answered, "I think we oughta open the casket. See how many arms we've got."

"How many arms?" The remark was offhanded in the cynical manner of professionals who deal with bodies and unreliable witnesses every day, and it skewered Davis. "What we've got is my father," he said with bitterness.

"Does he have to be here?" The coroner put the question to Ann Louise.

She looked at Davis. "Yeah, he stays."

As the coroner fumbled with screws, Davis stood off to the side and took an abrupt step away when he saw the lid begin to rise. He expected the hinge to make a gothic creak, but the swivel was noiseless. Ann Louise stood beside the coroner, and they both looked without bending forward, the way someone afraid of heights manages a view over the edge of a precipice.

"Well?" Davis asked.

"Everything's in order," the coroner said, already turning away.

Didn't he mean *disorder*? Wasn't everything in a state of decay? What the hell did he mean? What kind of lame-assed remark was that? Davis was moving steadily toward the casket when Ann Louise stepped in front of him.

"You don't want to do that."

"Do what? I just want to see this great 'order.' What's wrong with that?" He heard the tension in his own voice.

"Davis, there's nothing to see. Please." Ann Louise held him loosely by one arm but let go when he moved forward.

The air smelled of earth and old clothes, almost pleasant, like the parlors in old houses Davis remembered from childhood. He expected his father to be completely skeletal after eight years underground, but a leathery covering hid the bones of the face, though the eye sockets were empty and deep. Somehow, he was still recognizable as Davis's father. Davis would know him anywhere, even in the underworld, worm-eaten and rotting away.

"He's got two arms." The coroner's voice seemed to echo through ductwork down a great distance.

Davis looked at his father and saw his bony hands folded where his stomach used to be. "Yes. Two arms," he repeated.

"We're out here because you claim you found a human arm. You thought it was your father's. Well, it wasn't." The coroner was lining up the facts.

Sensing his movement toward the conclusion that Davis had made up or imagined the whole episode of finding the arm, Ann Louise interrupted: "Next step is to look in the bottom of the grave."

Davis heard her but couldn't move. His eyes were fixed on something black protruding from beneath the satin pillow under his father's skull. It gave off a dull sheen in the light of the afternoon sun. Leather? Plastic? Glancing back to see Ann Louise and the coroner in a heated discussion of what to do next, Davis reached into the casket and poked the object hard enough to make it slide into view. An audio cassette. Davis slipped it into his pocket just as Ann Louise touched him on the shoulder. He crumpled to the ground, gasping.

"Jesus, Davis. I told you not to look." She was kneeling beside him. "It's all right. It's all right," she said, pulling him into her embrace and stroking the back of his head.

Davis couldn't stop hiccuping for air. He had been caught in the act, tapped by the guardian of the dead. His father's hollow eyes spun before him, twin whirlpools. "He knows. He knows." Over and over, he said it. And Ann Louise counterpointed each time with "It's all right. All right."

CHAPTER 11

WHEN DAVIS'S LEGS gave way, one of them twisted beneath him and went numb. As Ann Louise helped him stand, he hobbled with an arm around her shoulders. Someone happening upon the scene could mistake him for a resuscitated corpse.

"Don't know what got into me. Shock of seeing my father like that, I guess." He was temporizing, trying to explain himself as the cassette in his back pocket bulged and tugged him down. He thought of it as a brick, a lead brick. Why didn't he leave things alone? No chance, now, to put it back, as he watched the coroner close the casket. How could they not have seen him take it?

"Maybe we should get you home," Ann Louise offered as he limped a half circle to keep facing her.

"If you're gonna look for more bones down there, I want to stay."

The argument between the coroner and Ann Louise over what to do next had apparently concluded in her favor. "I'm just waiting for one of the guys to bring a ladder. Shouldn't take long, but why don't you go up to the car and sit down?"

"I'm okay now." But his head was pulsating, and he couldn't get his foot to wake up. "One foot in the grave," he thought. "Can't play around with this stuff." He brushed at his pants to secretly check for the cassette. It was on the same side as the numbness. Trying to walk himself back into life, he paced the edge of the two graves, noticing that the thin wall between them had collapsed. One hole, now, for father and mother, man and wife. One hole in the putrefying earth. The purifying earth.

The coroner and his coveralled assistants stood near the backhoe, talking and sometimes gesturing in Davis's direction. The policeman had posted himself next to the coffin and was mottled by the shadows of budding limbs as the afternoon sun sank lower.

Davis heard the ladder before he saw it. Jangling on the shoulder of the backhoe driver who had fetched it from the sexton's building, the aluminum flashed among the trees. Ann Louise pointed down as the workman drew nearer, and he jabbed it into one end of the pit, rocking it a few times for stability. Then Ann Louise went down, the crown of her head bobbing out of view.

Time stalled while she was under, and Davis kept checking his useless watch. How much longer could she hold out in the breathless world of the dead? Maybe she had stumbled upon a tunnel leading further underground and had wound her way beyond return. She could be lying on the bottom, wondering why no one came to her rescue, the light above shifting in the roil of air. Too long. She had been down too long, but Davis couldn't make himself move. When she finally reappeared, he realized he had been holding his breath.

Poised near the top of the ladder, Ann Louise called to the officer: "Donnie, get the forensics team out here."

The coroner, who had been leaning against the backhoe, pretending disinterest, rushed forward. "What'd you find?"

"Bet a lot of money I just found Charles Winningham."

The coroner drew in a deep breath and huffed it out. "You're just trying to get me down the ladder, Detective." The last word sounded like a slur.

"You know, Ted, I figure if you were any good as a doctor, you'd be working on live people instead of hanging out in graveyards."

Davis listened to this exchange the way a stranger monitors an argument in a department store. In his mind, he scored the match in favor of Ann Louise and gave her the win when she climbed out of the grave and told the coroner he could "go down or go away."

Dr. Ted turned and put his first foot on the ladder with a look of weariness and resentment. Davis imagined him in a room filled with guns, polishing the stocks and barrels, pulling oily rags through the bores and chambers. Or maybe he was surrounded by pornography, videotapes and magazines. Maybe his invalid mother was in another room, calling his name, always calling.

Ann Louise watched the man with her hands on her hips, then turned to Davis. "Doing better?"

"Uh, yeah. I'm okay. Did you really find Winningham?"

"Found a skull just under the soil. I figure there's a body attached to it. If it's missing an arm, everything will begin to fit."

"Except how did Winningham get into my father's grave?"

"Most likely, someone put him there."

Davis thought of his father's coffin riding atop Charles

Winningham for the past eight years. It was another sea image, with Winningham paddling the dark waves, towing an odd boat. He would have borne Ralph Banks forever, the dead heft and steady dissolution of him, just Winningham and Banks in that bottomless sea of black. When Davis realized his father would be returned to the grave alone, adrift in that oceanic hole, a small terror swept him.

Everyone in the exhumation group had moved to the grave. Several sat on the ground for a better view of the coroner in the shadowed hole. He was down longer than Ann Louise had been, and when he came up, he gasped for words. "Nobody else goes down. This is now a homicide site and there's been too much tromping down there already. God knows how much evidence has been ruined." He was looking at Ann Louise but addressing everyone.

"Since when does the coroner's office manage homicide investigations?" Her voice was edgy. "This is my case, not yours," she continued, her breath coming harder. "And if I want to go back down the ladder, I damn well will."

Ted the coroner didn't look so much chastened as satisfied. He had lost the fight but managed to push his opponent past her limits. The pleasure he took in Ann Louise's lost composure made Davis mad. "You're a smug little bastard, aren't you?" he asked Ted, who shook his head as he walked toward the backhoe.

Ann Louise was sitting on the grass near the graves.

"Hey, at least you didn't have to shoot him."

Ann Louise laughed. "Don't think it didn't occur to me."

The wind had picked up and was making the branches clatter in the big oaks uphill. Davis looked toward them and saw someone step behind one of the trees. He locked onto the spot, waiting for the figure to reappear, but nothing moved. One of the men could have slipped away to piss in private, but all the members of the group were still in sight. Keeping his eyes on the tree, he paced up the incline.

Although the trees weren't leafed out and gave only a broken shade, the grove was cooler than the open area near the graves. He pretended not to be moving toward any particular tree but kept the exact one at the edge of his vision and, when the moment felt right, turned suddenly and walked to it. No one. He looked up into the mostly bare branches and then down. At the base of the tree lay five cigarette butts, all the same brand, all smoked down to the filter. When he looked downhill from this point, he could see the grave site clearly. Ann Louise was small and alone, her knees pulled against her chest. She could be mistaken for a sculpted headstone, melancholy fixed perpetually in marble; or for a spirit loitering in the late hours of the afternoon, a vision of grace.

A gust shuffled the branches and pushed Davis into the open. He picked up one of the filters, then let it fall, wiping his fingers hard against his pants. A commotion downhill drew his attention to the police van winding Greenwood's lane toward Ann Louise, who stood spooling it in, her right hand circling as if turning a crank.

The crew worked so efficiently that by the time Davis reached the graves, tripods for lights were being erected, orange and black wires running to the back of the truck. Ann Louise was giving directions as she helped unload metal boxes, and when everything was lined up neatly on the grass, she gave the signal to start the generator. Davis expected the sputtering to even into a full roar, but it never did. The sound kept vacillating, like a drill touching to bore and backing away, then again. "Do you really need the lights?" he shouted to Ann Louise.

She glanced at her watch and said something that sounded like "Dark being one," but which Davis interpreted as "It will be dark before we're done."

The first one back down the ladder was the coroner, this time with a satchel slung over one shoulder. Those crowded around the grave kept adjusting the tripod lights, apparently in response to the coroner's directions, and someone retrieved a huge flashlight from the van to hand over the edge. After Ted had been under for a few minutes, Ann Louise descended the ladder. Davis wondered which one was Virgil and which Dante. Didn't work because Ann Louise had to be Beatrice. She had no business in the underworld.

Davis ventured to the edge of the grave only once and could see very little—two people squatting in a game of marbles, each one brushing the soil for a better shot, picking up aggies and cat's-eyes. Most of the time, he paced between his father's coffin and the hole that grew more illuminated as the sun declined. Finally, the light surrounding the opening was brighter than anything else in the cemetery, and Davis hung back near his father's shadowed box.

When Ann Louise climbed into the upper reaches of the light and looked around for him, he knew he was invisible. Her eyes would have to adjust to find him leaning against his father, tête-à-tête of the living and the dead. He liked the feeling of being between worlds, so he didn't help her, didn't move at all. When she finally called his name, he answered with a single word that might have been a cough in the sputtering generator—"Here."

Squinting as she moved in his direction, Ann Louise snapped off latex gloves. "Shouldn't you get something to eat?"

Davis usually despised being reminded of his diabetes, even in oblique ways, but Ann Louise's concern didn't provoke him. "I will, as soon as you tell me what you've found."

"We'll have to tag and photograph everything, go through the whole routine. It's gonna take at least a couple of hours for us to get Mr. Winningham out of there."

"You're still convinced it's Winningham."

Ann Louise gave a tolerant smile. "Go eat. I'll stop by your mother's place to fill you in when we're done."

Davis protested only mildly. Ann Louise nudged him on, and soon he was walking among the twilit headstones. Each name seemed cut into darkness, and when he saw the rear window of his mother's car just beyond the cemetery wall, Gaylon's smeared word loomed like another family name. "Good old clan of Lier," Davis mumbled to himself. In the distance, the generator ripped the evening, and the glow from the graveside lights burnished the darkening air.

When Davis started the car, its rumble boxed him in. "This is what the generator sounds like inside the coffin." Foolish thoughts, he knew, but still they swarmed him. "Last time my father and mother will both be on the earth." He pictured his mother, hushed and patient in her little parlor at Berkley's, his father's bones resonant with the roar that ran the lights. Two boxes. Three, if you counted the car. Stupid idea. Dead is dead. You can't be mobile and be dead. Yet it was his turn. He was next in the order of things. "In the great disorder." He forced the alteration, then said aloud, with emphasis on each word, "Leave it alone," and jerked the car into the street.

While waiting in the drive-through line at the burger place, he pricked a finger and did a blood sugar check. 210. Not bad for a day of no monitoring. High but not in the panic zone. What the hell did it matter, anyway? Might as well binge on cheesecake and milk shakes and crawl into the coffin with his father or mother. Save the expense of another funeral. But he was already calculating how much insulin he would need to take when he got home. Shifting to reach for the bag when it was handed through the window, he felt the cassette press into his hip.

As soon as he entered the house, Davis knew someone had

been smoking inside. Odd how smokers believe they can fan the air or smudge out a butt and be undetected. His father had been a well-known secret smoker for years before his first heart attack. Davis would find him in the garage, a cloud slowly dispersing toward the rafters, the whole place stinking of tobacco, his father's breath bitter with it.

The smell evoked more nostalgia than fear, so Davis calmly closed the door and went into the kitchen with his burger and fries. When he loaded his syringe with insulin, he drew it full, 100 cc's, two days' worth, but this bolus wasn't for him. Holding the syringe like a knife ready for stabbing, he dropped his hands to his sides and called out, "Okay, Buford. Come on out and let me see you." Thinking of the hand clasping his chin and throat, of the cigarette filters crushed behind the tree, Davis waited for Ann Louise's jealous ex-husband to step from his dark corner.

Edging along the wall from the kitchen to the hallway, Davis began flipping on the lights. Bathroom, empty. Mother's bedroom, nothing. As he was about to turn off the light and close the door to his old bedroom turned storage area, he noticed something odd about the clothes hung on the line along one end of the room. Tilting his head to see around some boxes, he could clearly make out boots. Someone had sandwiched himself into the old clothes. "How does the story go from here?" he asked inside his own head, a question so vivid it seemed to have been spoken by someone else. Better to make the first move than to wait for Buford to garrote him if he turned to run. So he charged through the room, directly into the line of clothes, plunging in the needle and emptying it into the first solid thing he hit.

"Goddamn!" came a voice, and someone pushed hard and stumbled into the middle of the room. It was Haupt, the syringe hanging from his left bicep. "What the fuck have you done to me?" He was moving quickly toward Davis, the two of them knocking over stacks of old magazines and record albums.

Davis managed to get out of the room when Haupt fell, his feet tangled in some of the clothes knocked from the line. "You bastard!" he screamed as Davis slammed the door. But there was no lock and no way to block the door. All Haupt had to do was get to his feet. Hearing him scuttle amid the clutter, Davis jittered another needle into the insulin vial and filled a second syringe.

Haupt found Davis in the dining room on the far side of the table. "What did you stick me with, you little dickhead?"

"You'll know soon enough." Davis skittered one way and then another with each surge Haupt made around the table.

"You know how your mother died? You really want to know? I fucked her brains out. That's how she died. Who do you think you are, coming 'round to my house, bothering my family?" As he was saying "my family," Haupt lunged across the table, sliding into Davis just as another needle went in, this one in his upper back. For a moment, he seemed unable to get up from the jumble of chairs, but he rose with a fierce noise in his throat. "Damn," he said, wiping the sweat that now suffused him. "What'd you do to me?" He was beginning to shake violently.

Davis had backed out of the dining room and was standing near the front door when Haupt collapsed. He had given him enough insulin to produce a deadly reaction, but he felt an odd, almost scientific, detachment from the scene, even as he dialed 911 and told the operator to send someone prepared to handle severe insulin shock. After hanging up, he pulled a dining room chair near Haupt's tumbled body and observed.

CHAPTER 12

WHEN DAVIS TOLD the medics he had injected Haupt with 200 cc's of insulin, they exchanged incredulous looks. But there he was, a man exhibiting all the symptoms of a major insulin reaction. While one member of the team set up a glucose drip, the other injected glucagon. With the help of the policeman who was taking Davis's statement, the medics loaded Haupt's limber body into the ambulance and howled away.

"You say he was hidin' in the house when you came home," the officer repeated.

"Yes, in that back room where the old clothes and boxes are stored. And I knew someone was in the house because I could smell cigarette smoke. How many times do I have to tell you the same things?" Davis's tension was expending itself as exasperation. The last thing he needed was a cop who circled his cases like a cliché.

"How do you suppose he got into the house, sir?"

The officer had looked around for broken latches or windows and found nothing awry. Davis could tell him that Haupt had a key, but that would lead into matters involving his mother. So far, he hadn't admitted knowing Haupt.

"Look, I'm a diabetic, and I really need to eat. Is it possible for us to continue this conversation in the kitchen?" Davis was already moving in the direction of his cold burger and fries.

Flipping his notebook closed, the officer said, "I guess the rest can wait until tomorrow. Will you be here, sir?"

For a moment, Davis didn't know what the right answer was, but then he remembered. "Uh, no, I'll be at my mother's funeral. Berkley's."

"Very sorry for your loss, sir." And with that, the cop was gone.

As he prepared another syringe, Davis discovered he had used almost all his insulin on Haupt. He needed at least ten units for himself but could draw only a little more than six from the vial. To compensate, he promised himself he wouldn't eat all the french fries. Then he sat down at the kitchen table and devoured everything in the sack.

"Must have a death wish," he reasoned. "Or I was really, really hungry." He concluded it was better to be hungry to die than to die hungry. Haupt, if he were conscious, would be ravenous. The insulin surging through his blood in search of sugar to metabolize would make him want to eat the sheet the medics pulled beneath his chin. Davis had once devoured an entire box of assorted chocolates while sitting in the middle of his kitchen floor. He had found it covered with dust in the back of a cabinet above the sink, nuts and nougats and syrupy fillings, all of them stale. Didn't matter. The brain muttered, "Sugar," and the mouth fed.

The more he thought of Haupt, the more Davis regretted what he had done. His charge had been at Buford and was meant to even things between them. All Haupt's rage came after Davis stabbed him with the needle. Either the attack had infuriated him or the insulin had made him belligerent. What was it the kid who helped revive him at the airport had said? My daddy had a smart mouth, too, when the insulin whalloped him. Yes. Something like that.

Davis wandered the house, pondering hidden things. Haupt could have been after money. But Ellen Banks was far from wealthy, and she never would have kept money in the house, not any real amount. Then again, Ellen Banks wouldn't shack up at Howard Johnson's with a married man.

All the drawers in the bureau and dresser were closed. Closet doors were shut. Davis's old bedroom was too much of a jumble to give up any immediate clues. Maybe Haupt had just started his search when Davis came home. Playing out the scene as if he were Haupt, Davis pretended to enter the front door and stood for a moment drawing on his imaginary cigarette.

Where was the cigarette? All the ashtrays had been removed years ago. "Probably flushed it," he concluded, but when he lifted the toilet lid, he saw the bloody tissue from his morning finger prick still floating on the water. "Maybe the son of a bitch swallowed it," he said, dropping the lid in loud punctuation. "Field-dressed it and ate it. A real commando." He said this to his face in the mirror. Scalded by fluorescence, he looked every year of his age. Striking an oratorical pose, he gestured at his reflection and intoned, "The truth will set you free." As if in answer, the face in the mirror contorted the statement, "The truth will fret you. See?"

Damned right, he was fretting. And talking to himself. "My, how witty. Well, you always were a clever boy." The voice he used was as close as he could come to Tony Perkins's rendition of Norman Bates's mother. "Wouldn't hurt a fly." Then in his own voice, "But I'd shoot Sergeant Haupt full of enough insulin to kill three men." Lifting his chin to study his neck, he could still make out the pressure points of Buford's fingertips, a faint discoloration along the windpipe.

Narrowing his search to Haupt's hiding place, Davis entered what his mother called the dump zone. The only vestige of his old bedroom was the curtains, which had matched the bedspread and throw pillows, all of them in shades of brown. Sweet dreams of chocolate. The clothes Haupt had hid among hung from a sagging line running the full length of one end of the room. Dresses, coats, blouses, slacks, even an old one-piece swimsuit Davis recalled his mother wearing. She had been sitting on the edge of a pool at some little pink motel during one of their rare family vacations, striking what she called her Lana Turner pose. He was nine or ten and madly paddling in the deeper end.

In the corner closet, Davis found some of his father's clothes—shirts, a few suits, and several pairs of shoes. Reaching to brush away a cobweb, he tipped into the shoulders of the coats and caught an unexpected scent of him—Old Spice and tobacco and something else Davis couldn't identify, an almost floral fragrance tinged sour, like water in a vase. He inhaled and thought of the coffin, of the sunken grin on the still-recognizable face of his father. Eight years without air. When Davis clicked the closet door shut, it was the lid of another casket.

In a large box beneath one of the windows, he found photographs, hundreds of them still in the envelopes, just as they had come from the developer. All his mother's vows to organize them in albums had come to this, a jumble of poses, a past that could be sifted but never organized. There were people Davis didn't recognize, others he thought he knew but couldn't name. As he dug deeper, the years lost their color. Odd how the past looked so much more vivid in black and white, cleaner and simpler, purged of the clutter of the moment. Nothing left but the plainest recollection, the singular details. His mother and father stood out in sharp relief against a background of ocean, or hugging under mistletoe. Deceptive. Davis was there, too, from graduation gown to diapers. Flash, and the years were gone.

Wandering the room, Davis thumped his toe against suitcases, peeked into boxes of Christmas ornaments and old quilts. A croquet set was propped up in one corner, the mallet heads grass-stained and the striped balls scarred. Even the wire wickets were there, caked with a little dirt from the last game. All games blended in his father's fierce determination to win, his foot atop his ball, which rested against Davis's, and then the swing of his mallet, sending Davis bounding across the grass and into the neighbor's yard.

"It's a dump, all right," Davis said aloud to dispel the scene. Even the phonograph records, stacked waist-high in one corner, made him shake his head. LPs in their scuffed jackets, the nineteen-seventies faces of Herb Alpert and Merle Haggard. Tennessee Ernie Ford's Christmas album. That's what Haupt was after, some vintage vinyl. Could have been looking for "their" song. Then the thought of Haupt as a sentimentalist, blubbering in a corner while listening to George Jones moan out "He Stopped Loving Her Today," made Davis smile. "Yeah, right. Haupt and my mother were in *big* love."

Davis scanned the room one last time before shutting the door, then went to the living room sofa, bending halfway and letting himself drop. When he bounced against the cushion, he felt the cassette in his hip pocket. He pulled it out and studied it. Property of the dead. Technically, he was a grave robber.

The cheap, generic cassette was unlabeled, plain black. Why waste good money on something that was going to be shoveled under? To go for high fidelity, you'd have to believe in an afterlife with tape players. Standard issue for the dead, or maybe every soul with access to God's state-of-the-cosmos unit.

Fingering the tape as if he could hear what was recorded, Davis imagined it contained someone's last words to Ralph Banks, something that hadn't been said in life because of shyness or negligence. Pathetic to think of the driving need behind such a message to the dead. Or it could be a song. Dear God, it could be someone's idea of a final tune, "Feelings" or "Scarlet Ribbons." If something like that had been recorded for eternity, Davis didn't want to know. But the only way to find out was to listen.

After dropping the tape into the portable machine his mother had carried from room to room, he let his forefinger hover over the play button. No turning back once he punched it, like sending the rocket. He pushed down delicately and heard the machine engage. At first, the tape seemed blank. Then background noises, a rhythmic click. Then a woman's voice: "Oh, dear God! Please. Oh, God!" Her voice was husky, breathless. "Oh, God! Yes! Yes! That's it! That's it! Yes!" Davis stopped the tape.

"Jesus," he said aloud, realizing he was aroused and hating his body for responding. What the hell kind of tape was this? Pornographic? Having gone this far, he had to hear the rest of it. "Oh, yes, sweet baby. Come on. Come on." Then he heard a deeper voice grunting, a rhythmic rocking. "That's it. That's it. Oh, oh, oh!" And then silence.

Davis let the tape play to the end, hearing only blankness, and then flipped it to the other side. Nothing else there, either. Static of dust and emptiness. The house was quiet, except for the low drone of the tape player. When the machine automatically shut off at the end of the tape, he took the cassette and studied it again, hoping he had overlooked some identifying marks. Blank. Just eight or ten minutes of intercourse. No, of fucking.

No way to identify the man on the tape, so it could be his father or Haupt or John F. Kennedy. And the woman's voice was humped out of shape by the grit of the moment. Could be his mother or any woman. So many coupling possibilities, the whole world seemed to be screwing. And, of course, it was, at that very moment.

Shaking off the thought, Davis focused on the possibilities. The most benign was that he had just listened to his parents. If that were so, then his mother had left it in the casket as a kind of sweet, if kinky, memento for the dead. If it were his mother and another man, or his father and another woman, his mother still might have tucked it underneath the satin pillow during the final viewing. Could have been her way of taunting him beyond life, saying, "Take your goddamned infidelity with you" or "Take mine."

Maybe Haupt put it there. Had he been around that long? Pretty sick to screw another man's wife and then bury him with the evidence. Could that have been what Haupt was looking for? Maybe there were other tapes, all made by Davis's mother. What if it aroused them to record themselves? Wanting more than grunts and invocations of God, Davis made a cursory search for a cache of cassettes. He needed a name, a recognizable voice, but there were no other tapes.

Hoping fresh air would clear his head, he stepped out onto the front porch. The night was crisp by Tennessee standards but balmy to Davis, who was used to Iowa winters with hard freezes into spring. The lives around him were palpable, and he imagined he could hear the unintelligible drone of a hundred conversations. Friday night. End of the work week and payday for almost everyone. By now, they had gone for groceries, splurged on fast food for the family, or were on beer number four or five. "My people," Davis said, lifting his hands like an evangelical preacher.

He walked to the edge of the yard and looked up and down the overparked street. Not enough room in the driveways and garages for everyone's four-wheel drive or minivan, those second and third family cars, Grandma's or Junior's. Maybe Aunt Widow was staying for the weekend, her boxy Dodge doing its part to narrow the street to a single lane right in front of the house. Stupid to think he could see into their lives, feel even a distant kinship. No one here knew him. Worse, he didn't care.

The people he thought he knew best were turning out to be strangers to him. If he didn't know them, maybe he didn't know himself. Who he was, and what he had done with his life, were premised on being Ralph and Ellen Banks's son. Nice couple. Happily married. The kind of folks you'd want for neighbors and would be glad to give a spare key to your front door. How many times had his father said, "If a man isn't exactly what he seems to be, I don't want to know him"? Plain-spoken Ralph, screwing away the afternoon with some other woman. Modest Ellen, tangled in the motel sheets with Haupt. Decent people. "My people," Davis said again, this time barely muttering the words, feeling himself dissolve.

He closed the front door behind him. The air inside the house was still acrid from cigarette smoke. Haupt must have been there a long time, waiting for Davis or looking for something. This must have been how the place smelled when Haupt and Ellen shared a cigarette after sex. Davis opened front and back doors to make a draft through the house and swung wide the doors to all the rooms to let out any molecules of smoke breathed out by Haupt. Was it an exorcism or an act of purification? Davis pondered the difference but couldn't decide which. Malevolent spirits either way. When the breeze slammed the back door, Davis stepped outside to find a brick or a heavier prop. There, where Haupt had flicked them, were three cigarette butts.

When Ann Louise called through the opened front door, Davis was lost down such tangled, smoky passages that he thought his mother was summoning him. "Davis?" The name was a question, meaning not simply Are you home but Who the hell are you. True son of the South, named for the president of the Confederacy. No one had ever told him that. His mother claimed she just liked the name. Whatever her real reason, she bequeathed her son a legacy of place and history. In his heart, he had always felt proud of the name. Rootless, he had a place to look back to, a complex story still unfolding in which he was a character. He was one of the Southerners.

"Davis? Are you in there?"

As he stepped inside from the back steps, saying, "Come on in," he shuffled the weight of the past. Ann Louise was standing just beyond the threshold, an uncertain look on her face. "Come in," Davis insisted, motioning her forward.

"You all right?"

Hesitating, Davis replied, "That's a complicated question."

"Did you eat something?"

"Yeah. Maybe more than I needed." Then he remembered being out of insulin. "Know a drugstore that's still open?"

Ann Louise's tentative expression changed to serious concern. "What do you need? Insulin?" As she spoke, she guided Davis to the sofa.

"How's the archaeological dig going?"

"For God's sake, Davis, I'm trying to help you. Tell me what you need and I'll go get it."

"I'm out of insulin. The fast kind."

"I don't know what that means. How many kinds are there?"

Davis slowly brought himself up through the smoke and the grasping fingers of the dead. "Humalog. Just ask for the fast-acting kind."

"What about a prescription?"

"You're a cop; just flash your badge. Walk right up and buy it. Not really a drug, but that stuff can kill you, you know." Davis heard his clipped speech and knew he was exaggerating his condition. But it felt good to be attended to by Ann Louise. She was all tenderness and concern. She was on his side.

"You lie down and I'll be back in ten minutes. You hear me?"

Davis lifted his legs one at a time and carefully placed them side by side on the sofa. Closing his eyes, he said, "Okay." Then he lay quietly, thinking of Ann Louise rushing to his aid. The house now smelled of night air and Ann Louise, and Davis inhaled deeply, bobbing in and out of sleep.

CHAPTER 13

ANN LOUISE HAD closed the front door behind her, but the back one remained open, and a breeze drew through the house. Davis thought of it as a single strand of green, stitchery of spring, the beginning of a thin muslin that might cover him. Around the edges, a mockingbird made embroidery. Stupid, beautiful bird, fooled into song by a streetlight. Hidden in the heart of the dogwood, the bird outdid itself, pretending to be chickadee, cardinal, robin, and wren, shrilling like a bluejay, all in the artificial light. "Has to know the difference between night and day," Davis mused. "Has to be more than a jumble of songs." What was that old joke about the Englishman? Wake him in the middle of the night, and he'll talk just like you and me? Must be some way to startle the mockingbird into sounding like itself.

When the door swung open, Davis jerked upward on the sofa as if doused with a bucket of water.

"It's just me." Ann Louise's voice was reassuring but breathless. "Were you asleep?"

Davis swallowed wrong as he sat up, and a cough convulsed his throat. He wanted to say he was all right but couldn't find the wind for speech. When Ann Louise moved toward him to pound his back, he waved her off and bent himself double, clutching his ankles.

"Water?" Realizing the question couldn't be answered, Ann Louise headed to the kitchen as she asked it. When she gave the glass to Davis, he took it and set it down, sloshing the end table as his coughing shook him.

"It's all right." His voice was hoarse, barely audible. Worse than the spasmodic cough was his embarrassment. He wished Ann Louise would leave and come back later, when he would be composed, when he would be himself.

After the coughing subsided, she handed Davis the pharmacy bag containing the insulin.

Davis lined six boxes along the arm of the sofa. "Why so much?"

"I figured you'd go through one or two of those little things in no time."

When Davis laughed, his cough returned, and he threw back a quick drink of water. "Takes almost nothing to keep things going," he said, clearing his throat. I use a vial about every three weeks. You've bought a supply that'll last until August."

"Will it keep?"

Davis nodded as he focused on stopping another coughing spasm.

"Shouldn't you take a shot?"

Remembering that he had come up short with his injection for the burger and fries, Davis nodded again, making growling noises deep in his throat to stop the tickle. Retrieving a syringe from the kitchen, he opened one of the boxes of insulin and drew four units from the thumb-sized vial. Anne Louise studied him as he lifted his shirt and stuck himself in a pinch of flesh above the belt.

"Doesn't that hurt?"

With the syringe cap still clenched between his teeth, Davis mumbled, "Sometimes," thinking he should have checked his blood sugar before injecting the insulin. Too late to worry about it now, as the insulin swept down his veins.

Ann Louise looked different than she had when Davis left her at the cemetery. A change of clothes. She must have gone home after her work at the grave was done. Her exhaustion showed in the way she sat, giving herself to the soft cushions of the chair, seeping down as if she might finally submerge, her hands loose in her lap. Something in her fatigue made her more attractive—a fallen facade, maybe, revelation of the true Ann Louise, lovely in her weariness. Her eyes were focused softly on Davis.

"You must be beat. Have you had supper?" he asked.

"Yes and yes." Her answer was a lazy sigh.

"What we need is something to drink. Too bad my mother was a teetotaler." Then, remembering Haupt, he amended his remark: "At least I think she was." Propelled by that small doubt, he went into the kitchen and searched the cabinets, banging each door shut. On the top shelf above the stove, his hand touched something smooth, a curved secrecy. He stood on his toes to reach it and then could only wobble it out toward the edge, where it toppled toward him, a jug of burgundy.

Peeking around the doorway into the living room, he said,

"Looky what I found," and extended the jug. "I hear March was a pretty good month." He wiped dust from the jug's green neck and shoulders. Little more than a glass was gone; still enough in the bottle to make a glugging sound when poured.

Ann Louise drew away, wide-eyed, as Davis approached her with a water glass filled nearly to the top.

"Wait'll you see mine." He returned with a brimming iced-tea tumbler, and they both laughed.

"I'm not much of a drinker," Ann Louise said, warily studying the dark glass.

"Once you get it in your mouth, it usually goes on down." Davis demonstrated by taking a big gulp, holding it in a way that made his cheeks bulge, then swallowing. "Whoo, that's good as ditch water!" As soon as he said it, he remembered it was his father's expression, and he could see him downing his shot of whiskey every night before bedtime. "For medicinal purposes," he had always explained.

Ann Louise sipped cautiously at the brim of her glass. "I didn't think diabetics were supposed to drink."

"Pancreases aren't supposed to stop working, either. I figure it all evens out." The remark was a smart-assed backhand Davis had often used to fend off unwelcome attention to his disease, but he hadn't meant it in the usual way.

He was eager to change the subject. "So, how'd it go at the graveyard?"

Ann Louise held her glass with both hands, looking down at the reflection of her face in the unsteady circle of wine. "Got all the bones and other remains removed."

"And . . . ?"

"Found a wallet with Winningham's driver's license and pictures of his family. Even had fifty-seven dollars in it."

"You were right, then. You've found Charles Winning-ham."

"Looks like it. Can't say officially until Ted finishes his examination of the remains."

"You're being pretty cagey. Makes me think you're leaving something out."

"No, not really. It's just that Winningham is one for the books."

"Meaning?"

"Okay, get this. When we excavated the bones, they were in a little pit in the bottom of the grave, a place someone had dug out for the body. I'm guessing he was covered with only enough dirt to keep from being seen during your father's burial. We even found a little camping shovel between his legs."

"And if he hadn't tried to shake hands with me the other day, nobody would ever have found him. How was he killed?"

Ann Louise was slow to respond. "That's the kicker. We found an empty bottle of sedatives with Winningham's name on it."

"Somebody drugged him and buried him alive?"

"That's one theory. The other is that Winningham did it himself." When Davis said nothing, she continued, "He had a plastic bag over his head, black so it would be hard to see in the bottom of the grave. A rubber band cinched it tight around his neck. In every other way, he looked like someone who had just gone to bed. Pulled that cover of dirt over himself and went to sleep. Of course, the weight of the casket and vault did some damage, but mostly just pressed him into the earth."

"Seems an unlikely way to commit suicide."

"You wouldn't think so if you'd seen the remains. Not like any murder scene I've ever investigated. Too tidy. A calmness about the whole thing."

"Yeah, but aren't there meticulous murderers? Not every killer uses a lead pipe or a butcher knife."

"The coroner's report will tell us more, one way or the other."

"Will it tell you why no one saw Winningham when my father was being buried, or how a man can dope himself, put a plastic bag over his head, and then lie back in the dirt and die?"

"Well, we don't always get all the answers, do we?"

Because the subject made Ann Louise remote and seemed a part of her lethargy, Davis changed the subject. "How's the wine?"

"Mighty fine."

The rhyme made them laugh, and Davis said, "What we need is a little music." Vanishing into his old bedroom, he returned with a Brenda Lee album, concealed, to surprise Ann Louise. The needle fuzzed in its groove until it bumped into Brenda's voice: "There's too many rivers between you and me."

Ann Louise's face brightened. "You know, I used to think the words were 'There's two muddy rivers.'"

"I like that better," Davis proclaimed and began singing Ann Louise's version, adding other words of his own until he came to the line "We both killed the fruit on the vine." "That'd be what we're drinking," he said, taking a swallow.

Ann Louise lifted her glass and toasted, "To the killed fruit," and they both giggled, caught up in their own silliness. But when the cut of "I'm Sorry" started, they grew quiet, listening to Brenda's quavering voice plead for understanding.

"This was one of the songs I waited for—a slow dance. You remember those awful evenings at the gym in junior high?" Ann Louise smiled but said nothing, so Davis continued. "I was always too shy to do any of the fast dances, but I figured I could clutch and stumble as good as the next guy. Thank God for slow songs."

Ann Louise was on her feet, dancing with thin air until

Davis rose and stepped into her moving embrace. She felt smaller in his arms than he expected, almost fragile. They rocked back and forth in the narrow space of the living room between the coffee table and the other furniture, and when Brenda finished her song, they kept swaying and shuffling slowly as the record spun into silence, the needle clicking a steady cadence against the spindle. When they stopped and stood looking into each other's eyes, Davis felt as if they were still moving, spun by the night breeze. Their first kiss was little more than a touch, lips barely pressing. The next was longer, and Davis felt himself quicken as he touched her breasts. Ann Louise's arms loosely encircled his neck, and she let his hands move wherever they moved.

Saying nothing, Davis took her by the hand and led her to the only bed in the house, his mother's. In the dark, they slowly undressed each other, stopping now and then to kiss. When they were completely naked, they stood apart for a moment, breath coming heavily as though the oxygen had thinned. Davis felt Ann Louise's hand on him and steered her to the bed, an underwater slowness, his head humming from the depth of the dive. "Rapture of the deep," he thought. Then he said it out loud.

"Don't talk," Ann Louise whispered as she fumbled to stroke him. He moved from breast to breast, kissing her nipples, pinching them lightly with his lips as they grew more firm. She was breathing quickly, shifting herself beneath him, trying to put him inside her. But he was too limp. He could feel her rubbing against him, but nothing was happening. How could he want her so much and have nothing happen? He kept kissing and fondling, willing himself to grow hard; but the more he thought, the less rigid he became. A sad balloon. Party's over.

When he fell over to one side of Ann Louise and lay on his back, a light sweat breaking out on his forehead and chest, she turned to him and said, "Don't worry. It's all right." She brushed his hair away from his damp face and kissed him lightly on the cheek. "Really, it's okay."

"Was it as good for you as it was for me?" The question was said with such bitterness that Ann Louise drew back.

"Don't worry. These things happen."

"Yeah, these things happen—to diabetics. Looks like I'm due for a penile implant or one of those vacuum tubes Foster Brooks advertises in the diabetes magazines. Maybe a double dose of Viagra."

"For God's sake, your mother just died, and we're in her bed. It's really my fault. This was the wrong place, probably the wrong time."

Davis wanted to blame her but couldn't. The failure was all his. A real man could fuck in the middle of a goddamned family reunion, on the table with the potato salad and fried chicken. He almost said as much to Ann Louise but saw how the image debased the moment. Was this just a casual fuck? An attempted casual fuck, he should say. Shit, he thought too much. Why analyze everything to hell and gone. It didn't happen because it didn't happen. Comfort in tautology. Que será será, and other sappy slogans.

Ann Louise shifted closer and pulled his arm around her. "Can we just lie here awhile?"

Davis worried that she was patronizing him, even when she turned over and scooched herself against him. Spoons. Funny how automatically he slipped into position, drawing himself so close to Ann Louise he could feel the slight hairs at the nape of her neck against his nose and lips. "I'm not impotent," he said.

"Let's not talk about it. Everything's fine."

"I just have trouble now and then, especially when I'm under stress and my blood sugars have been all over the place."

"Shhh. I like just lying here with you."

Somehow it was all wrong. Every word she said was wrong. He knew she was trying to reassure him, hoping to dismiss his failure as something of no consequence, but her efforts made him feel worse. The more he tried to let the tension pass, the more it grew, until he bounded out of bed and began searching for his clothes in the darkened room.

"Davis, don't be like that."

"Like what? Limp?"

She was sitting now, the sheet pulled up around her. "Come on and lie down, just for a little bit." She patted the mattress beside her.

"Been there, haven't done that." The words were coming too fast, flashing their double edges. In a way, he wanted them to hurt her, but mostly he wanted to wound himself. "Hey, did you hear the one about the guy who couldn't get it up?"

"Yeah, he ran away and missed the best part of sex."

"Come on. Don't give me that bullshit. It's not about being close and cuddling; it's about humping and panting and coming. The godalmighty orgasm is the be-all and end-all. Everything else is either foreplay or fatigue."

"You can't really believe that."

"Can and do. What else would the point be? Did we dance our way back here and get horizontal just to neck? You can't tell me you're not disappointed."

"I'm disappointed in the way you're acting now."

"For Christ's sake! I despise being schmoozed. I'd have a lot more respect for you if you'd just give it to me straight. Ha! Did you hear that phallic reference? *You* give it to *me* straight. I sure as hell couldn't give it to you. The wimpy little noodle kept bending over."

Ann Louise moved to the edge of the bed and began to gather her clothes, pulling on panties, fastening her bra. "I'd better go."

"Yeah, right. Better move on out of here, now that you know the score. No score tonight. Zero. Nothing to nothing." Davis was laughing and moving erratically around the room. He had one sock on his foot and the other pulled over his hand and was gesturing wildly, a puppet show run amuck. "Swear to God, I don't know why you came over here. What did you expect to find? Nobody lives here anymore. Didn't you know that?" His breath was coming harder, and when he squatted in the middle of the room, rasping coarsely, Ann Louise knew he was in trouble.

"You took too much insulin, didn't you? Davis, what should I do?"

His eyes were fixed on nothing, and his shuddering breath was his only response. He had skidded out of the lanes of language. Too late to say that a jar of preserves, anything sweet would do. When Ann Louise rushed back from the kitchen with the sugar container and fed him heaping teaspoons, he couldn't swallow them. The grains coagulated and rolled from the corners of his mouth. He did better when she dumped sugar into a tall glass and filled it with water, stirring hard with a table knife. Davis took the crude solution blindly and swallowed the contents in three long gulps, even the sediment at the bottom. He kept swallowing as long as Ann Louise mixed them, until his eyes began to move around the room and he slurred, "What's going on?" Looking around him, Davis felt consciousness return, a slow seepage throughout the body. "Oh, Jesus." For the first time, he felt the glass in his hand, the coarse sugar granules on his lips and around his teeth. Ann Louise was crouched beside him, wearing only her underwear. "I'm sorry. I'm sorry."

"Are you all right?"

He looked at her so long without speaking that she asked the question again. "Yes. Thank you. Oh, Jesus, I'm sorry." The apology was not so much for the insulin reaction as for the disease itself.

Ann Louise helped him stand, and after she got him into bed, slid in behind and pulled up close, repeating, "It's all right. Everything's all right." Her words were palpable against his neck, warm touches of breath seeming to travel down his spine until he was suffused with Ann Louise and fell asleep.

CHAPTER 14

LYING CHILLED AND alone beneath a single sheet, Davis might have been in the morgue. His thoughts were shards of a scene he couldn't immediately reconstruct, so he lay immobile, wondering if he could move. The more he focused on lifting an arm or sliding a leg from beneath the sheet, the more leaden he felt. Deadweight. Dead. Stupid idea. He was breathing, lying in his mother's bed. His dead mother. But even after the powdery dream had blown away, he pretended he was dead. There was the ceiling, dull white above him, the underside of infinity. He closed his eyes and exhaled all his breath, waiting until his lungs forced him to accept the air again.

The gritty sweetness in his mouth called back the end of the evening, and his failure. "Way to go, stud," he said, looking down at his penis, which bulged beneath his pants, half erect from the pressure of his bladder. As he sat on the edge of the bed, he considered that he might be half dressed or half undressed. "Half-cocked is more like it. Definitely half-socked." He extended his legs and studied his one bare foot, thinking how symbolic it was to be half dressed in either direction.

The sun was up, but the day was overcast. A light rain had fallen sometime during the night, deepening the dark street, beading the grass. Davis was fumbling in the bathroom when the phone rang. He counted seven rings before silence. Nobody he wanted to talk to. No need to talk. Words seemed useless. This would be a day of useless words. Nothing that mattered could be said in the face of death, in the unresponsive face of his mother decked out in her blue dress for the subterranean silence.

When the phone insisted again, he worried that someone would come to check on him if he didn't answer. Nothing would be worse than Aunt Goldie's simpering face at his front door.

"Are you all right?" It was Ann Louise. Somehow, Davis hadn't thought she would be the caller. Wasn't last night enough for her? What more proof did she need, unless she was thinking of taking him on as a project: the resurrection of Davis Banks. "Davis?"

"Right here."

"Sorry I had to leave before you woke up. This Winningham thing has got me going in circles. Can you come down here—to the station, I mean? There are some things we need to talk about."

Was she really going to revisit their pathetic encounter of last night? No way was Davis prepared for that conversation. "Uh, I don't think there's anything else to say. Inaction speaks louder than words." The self-deprecation was his disguise, his way of hiding in plain view.

"I mean about Winningham. We need to talk about him and some other things. Aren't you at least curious to know what we've learned?"

So it was all business now. Detective Wilson on the line. "Give me an hour," Davis said, about to hang up when he heard Ann Louise's voice at arm's length.

"Why didn't you tell me about the intruder? I gave you every chance last night."

"Well, something else came up—or didn't."

"Any idea why he was in your mother's house?"

Davis paused, thinking he would tell Ann Louise the whole story of Haupt, but it was too complicated, and he wasn't in the mood. "Probably one of those burglars who finds his jobs in the obituaries."

"In case you're interested, he's going to be all right. They'll keep him in the hospital for a few days for observation. Are you going to press charges?"

"Don't think pressing works very well with me."

Ann Louise hung up, leaving Davis to wait for the dial tone, then the off-the-hook wail. She had known about the Haupt episode all along, had been testing him, letting him fail her again. Maybe he was on her list of suspects in Winningham's death.

•

When he entered the station, Davis smelled coffee and knew he needed to eat. Whatever his blood sugar level might be, he was hungry, so he was glad to find Ann Louise standing near her cubicle at a little table offering bagels, doughnuts, and cinnamon buns. He had slipped several syringes and one of the bottles of insulin into his pants pocket. As he approached, he flashed the small vial and motioned toward Ann Louise's desk, where he could inject himself without attracting attention. She stayed near the table, keeping a casual lookout, and when he walked over, she asked, "Are you okay?"

"Well, you know how it is. Night of carousing with the ladies."

Ann Louise didn't laugh or even acknowledge the remark. Instead, she walked to her cubicle. Davis followed and sat at the corner of her desk, a bagel with cream cheese balanced atop his cup of coffee as he scooted the chair around. "So, what gives, Detective?"

Ann Louise took a deep breath and then entered the official role he was forcing on her. "We've got preliminary tests back from the coroner. It's Winningham, all right."

"Great. Got your man. Good for you, Detective."

"Look, Davis, can we drop the sarcasm? I'm not in the mood for it. What happened last night happened. Okay?"

"Hey, can't argue with that kind of logic."

"Shit. Just let up a little, will you? You might learn something."

Davis felt too uneasy to cooperate completely. His wise-cracks were his only cover. To give them up was to stand exposed again. He imagined his penis, small in the folds of his briefs. "Let the lesson continue."

Fixing him firmly with her gaze, Ann Louise said, "Dental records for Winningham match the teeth we found. That makes the identification a dead certainty."

Dead certainty. Certainly dead. The phrase mutated and spread through Davis's brain, making him smile.

"What's so funny?"

"Nothing. Go on. Got anything else to teach me?"

"Goddamn you, Davis. I said to lighten up. If you don't

stop the smart-ass stuff, I'll get somebody to show you the door."

Davis smiled more broadly, thinking of doors and entries and failures; but he forced himself to stop. "Okay. You're right. Go ahead."

"We were able to lift some fingerprints from the prescription bottle and the handle of the shovel. Most of them were Winningham's."

"Who left the other ones?"

"The pharmacist, the guy at the hardware store who sold Winningham the shovel, who knows?"

"Maybe the person who murdered him?"

"It's not a murder, Davis. Nothing about the remains suggests a struggle or any kind of attack. Charles Winningham put himself in the bottom of your father's grave, took those pills, bagged his head to suffocate himself, and waited for the weight to come down on him."

"But somebody could have slipped him the pills and put him there. That has to be at least a possibility, doesn't it?"

"All the evidence points to suicide."

"Okay, then, as far as you're concerned, Charles Winningham killed himself, and you solved the mystery. Case closed."

"Not really closed. There are questions we need to answer."

"Seems to me you have all the answers."

"Every death is the end of a story, but the ending doesn't always make sense until we have the rest of the story."

"Jesus, that sounds like something I might say to a sophomore literature class. If you ever want to swap jobs for a few weeks . . ."

"Don't you want to know why Winningham chose your father's grave?"

"Well, let's see—it was available. How's that?"

"So you're content to think of it as a random choice? Might as well have been another grave in another cemetery?"

"Why not?"

"What if Winningham knew your father?"

"My father was a shift supervisor at Trane Manufacturing. He didn't hang out with many lawyers."

"Still doesn't mean they couldn't have known each other. Clarksville's not that big."

"Wait a minute. I see where this is going. You want to play out the Romeo and Juliet plot, only with two men instead of a couple of horny teenagers. You think Winningham killed himself in despair when my father died, because . . . hell, I don't even want to finish the thought." But he had finished it in his head, where it tumbled like a clump of garbage swept downstream.

"I don't believe in randomness where suicides are concerned. People kill themselves for specific reasons and in well-chosen places. Suicide is the irrational conclusion to a line of rational thinking."

"They teach you that at some police seminar? Christ almighty! What if Winningham just wanted to vanish, wanted to leave a mystery behind? He could have planned for a long time and just happened to choose my father's grave. The scheme would have been more important than the particular place. All that mattered was pulling it off. Death by disappearance. Has a certain appeal, don't you think? Anyhow, I'm still holding out for murder."

Phones were ringing all around them, a twittering grove. Davis sipped his coffee and waited for Ann Louise's answer, which was a piece of paper pushed across the desk. "We found this in Winningham's wallet."

After wiping his fingertips on his pants, Davis pulled the

little square toward him. A newspaper clipping. His father's obituary. "And this would prove what?"

"You don't find it odd that the man buried under your father had your father's obituary in his pocket?"

"Apart from the irony, you mean?"

"So, this is just a coincidence." Ann Louise was beginning to sound like a grammar school teacher who couldn't understand her pupil's thickheadedness.

"If Winningham was planning to kill himself, he probably clipped this from the newspaper so he'd know when and where to go with his bottle of pills and his shovel."

"Come on, Davis. You don't think he could have remembered that Ralph Banks was being buried in Greenwood Cemetery two days after this notice was published?"

"How the hell do I know what kind of memory the man had? He was a lawyer. Maybe he was a demon for documentation."

"Davis, I'm looking for the story that leads up to the ending we've discovered. If Winningham and your father were having a relationship, Winningham's decision to kill himself and be buried with your father makes sense. Everything falls into place."

"And if they didn't know each other, if the grave was randomly chosen, how does that screw up your narrative?"

"You're forgetting that I followed this case eight years ago, even though I wasn't one of the investigators. And I've gone back and looked at the file. One of the things that came out in the papers and led to a lot of gossip was Winningham's homosexual activities. We've got statements from some of the men who knew him. Knew him in *that* way."

"Got anything in the file that says my father was one of Winningham's lovers?"

"It's just hard to account for Winningham's suicide any other way. He was well off, had a good legal practice, a nice home. You've seen the house yourself."

"Had a nutty wife, too. Or wasn't she allergic to the world back then? Maybe she killed him."

"Well, there's no point in going any further with this."

"How much further could you go? You've started with the speculation that Winningham killed himself, and followed that up by assuming he did it in my father's grave because the two of them were lovers. Ever consider writing cheap novels?"

Ann Louise stood and looked at her watch. "I've got to check with the coroner again, and then we need to get your father reinterred."

His father. Davis hadn't even thought about his father. For eight years he had been dependably underground, but now he was out in the world once more. "Where's the coffin?"

"Coroner's in charge of it. Said he wanted to check for anything we might have missed."

"He's not going to do anything to my father, is he? I mean, he can't without my permission, right? That can't be legal."

"The court order for the exhumation gives him the right to do whatever he thinks is necessary, but I doubt he'll touch your father's body."

Davis was thinking of the cassette recording and wondering if anything else might be hidden in the casket. Could be photographs of Ralph Banks and Charles Winningham going at it in the Ramada Inn. No, he couldn't let himself think that way. His father was as straight as Davis himself. Bad comparison after last night's poor performance. And Davis kept hearing the woman's voice on the tape. What if it was his mother with another man? She could have been driven to affairs by his father's indifference to her, by his preference for men. If that were true, placing the tape beneath his head would have carried a double load of bitterness.

"I want to see my father." Davis's tone was matter-of-fact, as if his father were waiting in a holding cell and could speak with him.

"I don't think that's a good idea."

"Oh, that's right, you're afraid of Dr. Ted. Sorry, I forgot that little wrinkle." The ploy was transparent, but he didn't have any other leverage with Ann Louise. He certainly couldn't wink slyly and say, "For last night's sake, sweetheart."

Ann Louise stood without speaking, then turned suddenly and said, "Follow me." They walked out of the station and entered through a plate-glass door two buildings down the street. Downhill. A guard in the entryway said, "Mornin', Detective," as Ann Louise passed, pulling Davis in her wake. When they reached the rear of the building, Ann Louise made Davis wait while she went through a set of swinging hospital doors, the kind found in emergency rooms.

What emergency could arise in a morgue? A little post-mortem twitching might make the nightman jumpy, but who would hit those doors with a gurney, yelling "Stat!"? When Ann Louise didn't return right away, Davis eased his way inside and followed the voices.

On a stainless-steel table at the end of a green room awash in bright light lay something twisted, compressed like a bundle of roots in shrink-wrap. "Winningham," thought Davis, but as he looked around, he saw his father's coffin, empty. "What the hell's going on here?" he challenged, bulling his way across the room.

Ann Louise was saying his name over and over, and the coroner was yelling, "Get out of here! Now!" But Davis was uncontrollably drawn to the table, to the small body of the man who had been his father. He was shrunken to half his size, completely stripped of his clothing. The room smelled of formaldehyde and backwash land after the water has dried up.

"Daddy?" Davis was standing against the table, looking down at the husk, at what could have been half man/half locust. "The pupal stage," he thought. Then he realized he was looking at the arches of the pelvic area. His father's penis was gone. "What have you done to him, you son of a bitch?" He had turned on Dr. Ted and was backing him across the room when Ann Louise grabbed one of his arms and twisted it behind him, tipping his whole body forward. The more he struggled, the harder she bore down, until his arm was electrified with pain. When he hit the swinging doors, head lowered like a goat's, Ann Louise gave him a push and let him go.

"What kind of pervert is he?" Davis had his back to the wall and felt his legs give way beneath him. "Don't let him do that to my daddy, please. Please don't let him." The sobs rose in him like huge bubbles, bouncing his whole body with each release. "Oh, God, why is he doing that? Don't let him. Don't let him."

Ann Louise knelt beside him, repeating his name until he looked at her. Then, very deliberately, she said, "I'll take care of it. Right now. Okay?"

Something in her face calmed Davis. He believed her, knew she would stop what the coroner was doing. Somehow, she would stop him.

"You stay here. Understand?"

Even if he had wanted to get up, Davis wasn't sure his legs would support him. So he slumped against the cold cinder blocks for what seemed a long time, daubing his eyes with his shirtsleeve. He tried to imagine what Ann Louise and the coroner were saying to each other and wished she would put Dr. Ted in an arm hold and bang his head into the wall. Maybe she would take out her pistol and study it while making veiled threats. Was she capable of that?

When she came through the swinging doors, she was perfectly composed. "Come on. Everything's all right now. Your father's back in his coffin, and we'll rebury him this afternoon."

Unsteady on his feet, Davis touched the corridor wall at intervals as they left the building. The morning air immediately made him feel better. Then, without warning, he vomited.

Ann Louise placed an arm around his shoulders and handed him a tissue from her jacket pocket. "Come on, let's get you away from here. Nothing to be sorry about," she said, as Davis kept saying he was sorry. "Is your blood meter in your car?"

Davis nodded, feeling the acid in his throat, and nodded again when Ann Louise asked if he had parked in the uphill lot.

When they reached the car, Ann Louise retrieved the monitor from the backseat and handed it to Davis, watching him as he pricked a finger and placed a blood drop on the little strip. The countdown from forty-five seconds to the result—330—left them staring at each other.

"You need a shot, don't you?"

Davis nodded and fumbled the vial and syringe from his pocket. He calculated that three or four units would do, then stuck himself in the fleshy part of his stomach.

Ann Louise winced and said, "I've gotta get back to the station. Will you be okay now?"

He answered yes but knew it was a lie, at least in the long run. He would definitely not be all right. No one would be all right. When he looked in the side mirror, he saw his father's shrunken face.

CHAPTER 15

When Davis parked in front of Marie Winningham's, he tried to remember driving there but couldn't. No turns, no stoplights, just the straight route of his intent. Marie Winningham might have a portion of the truth, and Davis had fixed his mind on her as a stricken man grasps the wheel and focuses on the emergency room. If she couldn't mend him, she might at least commiserate.

When no one answered the doorbell or the knocks, Davis stabbed against the wood with the thick side of his fist. Then he wandered around the house, trying to see movement inside. The ground was matted with years of unraked leaves, but scrappy grass showed where wind had whipped clear spaces. A few jonquils thrust yellow-green blades through the deepest mulch.

When he rounded the house and started along the back side, Davis heard talking. Tilting an ear toward the shuttered window, he picked up disconnected bits of a voice: ". . . more healing . . . lost connection with . . . drift with your breath to . . ." A man's voice, rhetorically polished, almost histrionic.

Davis continued along the outside wall, trying the kitchen door, thinking he would explain himself after getting inside. He didn't have time for quirkiness or shyness. He needed answers. When he pushed the rear garage door, it opened to a Volvo, new under its layers of dust, but not a recent model. The last person to drive it was probably Charles Winningham. On the other side, against the overhead door, black trash bags were piled floor to ceiling, spilling toward the center of the room. Lifting one, Davis was surprised by its lightness. Inside, he found only sandwich bags, hundreds of them, crumpled. The same with every other trash bag he opened.

The door to the kitchen was unlocked but wouldn't give until Davis bumped it with his shoulder. A wide arc on the linoleum showed where the door had dragged for years. Pulling up on the knob as he pushed kept it from stuttering across the floor.

The kitchen at first appeared to be immaculate, but then Davis realized it was simply lacking signs of habitation—no dishes, knickknacks, curtains. Surfaces were steel-wool-scoured, but the room looked unused. He stood in front of the sink, studying his thin reflection in a pane of the window. A place for ghosts, spare spirits of the scraped and stripped-down world of Marie Winningham.

Where a table should have been in the adjoining dining room, Davis found only space, a small ballroom, if anyone cared to dance. Beyond, in the center of the house, was the room with the stone fireplace, where he and Ann Louise had tried to talk to Marie. Resonant here was the voice he had heard from outside, clearer now: "Listen to your blood. You can hear it moving through your veins, a steady flow. Listen. Listen to your breath. Let it slow. Let yourself drift on your own blood."

He followed the voice to a closed door at the end of a short hallway. "Imagine how clean the stones are in sunlight, the stones in the middle of the stream, the stones in the harbor of yourself." Louder now, just beyond the door, "This is your central purity, the crystal essence. Look around. Imagine it. Breathe the deep, clear air of it."

Quietly opening the door, Davis was dazzled by light, crumpled and broken refractions from all directions. Eyes closed, Marie Winningham balanced on a wooden stool, listening to the taped voice. She was wearing a dress several sizes too big for her. Bleached white, it was shapeless, as if it had been pounded with stones. Around her, the walls were hung with aluminum foil, the ceiling likewise covered. Sensing his presence, she looked directly at him, tipping a moment on the stool before screaming and running to a corner tented with plastic. Davis tried to explain himself, but still she screamed, while the taped voice held its complacent tone.

"I'm with the police, Mrs. Winningham. Remember me from yesterday? The police." He kept repeating these simple words in various combinations until the screaming stopped and the blurred figure behind the plastic ordered him to leave. "I need to ask you a few more questions. Please, Mrs. Winningham. We can do it here or down at the station."

A long silence followed. Then she slipped through a flap in the plastic and pulled sandwich bags onto her hands as she quivered forward.

"Do you know we've found your husband's body?"

"I don't have a husband. I don't have anybody." Fumbling with her makeshift gloves, she made little cuffs by tucking the ends under.

"Do you know where your husband went when he left?"

Marie backed up until she was touching the plastic sheeting but didn't answer.

"Did your husband ever mention the name Ralph Banks?"

"Ask him."

"You don't seem to understand. Your husband is dead. We found his body yesterday."

"The air's no good. You've ruined the air." She was back inside her translucent corner, and Davis could see her fitting an oxygen mask over her face. Then the thrush and click of the machine obliterated his questions. He wanted to pull her from her veiled space and force her to listen to him.

Stopping just outside the plastic wall, he whispered, "Are you crazy, Mrs. Winningham?" The question was ridiculous. A part of being crazy is not knowing it. Then again, maybe self-knowledge is the crazy person's one point of lucidity. He asked again, in a louder voice. No reply. "Was your husband crazy? Was he the kind of man who would kill himself and try to hide his own body?" Realizing one thing didn't logically follow the other, Davis said in a softer voice, "I mean the other way around." What a joke, talking nonsense to a silhouette on oxygen. The taped voice was saying, "You are a whole person. Focus on your wholeness." Imitating the soothing tone, Davis said, "Of course, you're crazy, completely crazy, but that's a kind of wholeness." Then he was gone, down the hallway and out the front door.

The mail carrier was crossing the lawn when Davis stepped onto the porch. "Mornin'," he said as he shuffled an armload of envelopes. For a moment, Davis struggled to reenter the real world, the everyday place where people went about their lives.

Inside, Marie Winningham was cornered in a room wrapped in foil, packed away like a leftover. But here was a man moving through the familiar steps of an ordinary day.

When he stepped forward to put his delivery into the box, Davis said, "I'll take those to Aunt Marie."

Pausing to study him for a moment, the carrier handed the small bundle to Davis and ventured a question. "How's your aunt doing?"

"Do you know her?"

"Not hardly. Been on this route over five years and never seen her. In fact, you're the only person I've ever seen at this house."

"But you know about her."

"I'm not one to talk about folks. Wouldn't want anybody talkin' 'bout me, but they say she ain't been the same since her husband disappeared. That was before I started with the post office."

Davis wanted to extract more information but couldn't think of the right questions to ask, so he started talking. "It's a sad situation. I haven't seen Aunt Marie but twice since Uncle Charles left. She was bad the last time I was here, but she's talking crazy now. Lots of stuff about murderers and her being warned to keep her mouth shut."

The carrier shifted his leather bag from one shoulder to the other and said, "They was people had reason to kill Charles Winningham, or so I'm told."

"Well, my uncle wasn't a saint; I know that. Might even go so far as to say he was a little twisted, if you know what I mean."

"I know exactly what you mean. Son of a bitch was—excuse me, didn't mean to use that term. I'm sorry. He was your uncle." Embarrassed, the carrier turned to walk away, but Davis stopped him.

"The way I hear it, some guy named Banks was tied up in it."

"Beg pardon."

"Banks, Ralph Banks, I think was the name. You know—him and Winningham."

"Could be. I just moved here from Ashland City about five years ago. But people still talk about Winningham. And the ol' lady—I mean your aunt—is . . . well, nobody never sees her, and you know how people go on. No offense intended."

"That's all right. You have a good day, now." Davis gestured with the mail clenched in his right hand and turned as if he were going back inside. The carrier shrugged under the weight of his bag and kicked off through the leaves.

Not a first-class envelope in the bunch. Everything was a solicitation or blind mailing. Half of the eight pieces were addressed to occupant. Davis didn't know what he had expected to find but felt disappointed as he clunked the bulk mailings into the box just outside the front door. Should have asked the mailman if anyone ever wrote to Aunt Marie. No, bad question, because even he didn't write to his weird aunt. The carrier might know that. Got to be careful how the story spins out. No knots in the thread. No dropped stitches. Could preface the question by saying, "I'm not much of a letter writer myself, but surely other people write to my aunt." That would do it. Why hadn't he thought quickly enough?

Lifting his wrist and the broken crystal of his watch, Davis realized he had mindlessly put it on when he dressed, even though its hands had crash-landed in the vicinity of twelve-thirty. "Couldn't be later than eleven," he thought, reading the overcast sky. Nothing to do now but go home and get ready for the funeral. No point in chasing down the mailman or trying to get Marie Winningham to make sense. Nobody knew anything, or there was nothing to know. Either way, he was snared by questions, their little hooks digging in and holding firm.

•

As he neared his mother's house, Davis noticed a Fort Campbell sticker on the rear bumper of a car parked at the curb. Lots of army base stickers around Clarksville, nothing at all out of the ordinary, but this one might be on Haupt's car. The thought clarified as Davis turned into the driveway. Haupt would have driven himself from the base, and his car would still be wherever he had parked it. He sure as hell didn't drive away in it. Jogging back to the car, Davis convinced himself it was Haupt's. The doors were locked, but he could see things piled on the backseat when he put his face close to the window and held his hands like blinders to cut down on the glare. Boxes tossed amid plastic bags. Might be things Haupt had taken from the house. "Damn him!" Davis said, his breath fogging the glass.

Working with a straightened coat hanger retrieved from the house, he was able to snake between the glass and the rubber insulation at the top of the driver's window. Contorting himself and bending the wire until it went down true, he snagged the lock and was inside. The air in the car was stale with tobacco. Davis scratched through papers in the glove compartment until he found a registration slip. "The good sergeant," he said to his left eye in the mirror.

With both front windows rolled down, Davis pulled the largest box onto the front seat. Tucked shut, the top sprang open when he pulled on the middle of the flaps. A woman's coat. Charcoal. In the smaller boxes were black pumps and toilet items, including a blow-dryer and a small mirror with magnification on one side and normal reflection on the other. Davis held it close, until his face was so near it was unrecognizable. The plastic bags held a nightgown, bathrobe, slippers.

Haupt was not stealing these things. He was trying to return them. They were the personal effects of Ellen Banks, the things she had with her when she died. Haupt must have thrown them into the car at the Howard Johnson's and then packed them later for return. He had probably let himself into the house to prowl around a bit and make sure he could safely unload his secret cargo. Or was the dirty bastard putting together a hoard of memories to cart away? Was Haupt coming or going? Davis tried hard to remember seeing any of the items in his mother's house. The coat? The blow-dryer, maybe?

Pulling the backseat loose from its brackets, he peered into the trunk. Too dark to see what was there, so he crawled through and felt his way around, his hand finally touching canvas. A duffel bag. He dragged it with him as he climbed back into the car. Haupt's necessities: shaving kit, socks, underwear. The son of a bitch was ready to roll. All he needed was a woman. Ellen Banks. Any woman. Ellen fucking Banks.

•

Davis unpacked the parcels. The coat was easy to hang in its usual place, but he fumbled with the nightgown and bathrobe, finally jamming them into a bureau drawer. The pumps dropped neatly among the shoes; the toiletries had places on the dresser or in the bathroom. A hair-spray spritzer fit exactly inside a little circle in the dust.

Putting things back made Davis feel better, but the process didn't make his mother whole. Instead, it fractured her into Haupt and motel beds. Checking the bags to be sure he hadn't missed anything, he withdrew something soft, silky, a pair of panties. When he realized what they were, he dropped them, then felt foolish when he couldn't force himself to pick them up. Haupt might have taken them off her himself, before they climbed into bed, before her heart attack. Trying to stop the scene from playing in his mind, Davis kicked the panties underneath the bed.

Why did everything keep coming back to sex? Sex and death, the odd twins. You reproduce and then you die. Pretty simple. And here was Davis Banks, the only thing Ralph and Ellen had to show for all their efforts, their puny bid for immortality. Well, maybe not the only thing. Haupt and Winningham had to be factored in. Humping with the oldies. Hell of a way to remember his parents.

To slow his plummeting thoughts, Davis began unpacking his funeral clothes. His black suit came crumpled from the suitcase, and when he tried to hang it over the hall doorway, it dropped to the floor and picked up enough lint to make a universe. Brushing simply rearranged the constellations. To get the wrinkles out, Davis hung the coat and pants in the bathroom and turned on the shower. Hot water only, full blast, to make steam. He closed the door and went back to his suitcase for a shirt, socks, and clean underwear, paced the hallway for a few minutes, and then retrieved the suit. None of the wrinkles were gone but the cloth had definitely relaxed, gone limp, in fact. "Perfect," Davis said, turning the coat one way and then another. "Absolutely perfect."

When he was dressed, he tried to wipe away the lint with a damp washcloth, but managed only to make the suit feel clammier. "Don't want to compete with the corpse," he thought, then chastised himself for the insensitive joke at his mother's expense. "Careful, or you'll offend yourself." Leaning in toward the mirror as he wound his tie around, he repeated the word "careful," forming it slowly, watching his lower lip flip out from beneath his front teeth.

When he was ready to go, he checked the clock in his mother's bedroom. Just twelve forty-five. Too early to put in an appearance at the funeral home. Much too early to put up with Aunt Goldie. But there was nowhere to sit without collecting more lint. Better to stay upright. Maybe a walk around the grounds.

The backyard was spongy from the night's rain, the grass tall enough to dampen the toes of Davis's shoes. The sun flickered now and then through thinning clouds. Good day for a funeral. The only kicker was that the burial would have to wait until tomorrow. His father would be reinterred today. A double burial was a bigger return for the price of his plane fare than he had ever imagined.

The stupid monologue wasn't working. Davis kept thinking of his mother, her panties in Haupt's hand, Haupt mounting her, the groaning, "Oh, God! Yes!" But who would be on top when his father was paired with Winningham? Was his father dominant or submissive? Giving or receiving? He couldn't decide where to put his father.

Desperate to stop such thoughts, Davis found himself pulling on the lawn-mower cord, the engine coughing and then catching. Just one full strip down the lawn and it choked on the wet grass, but the air was sweet with bruised green, the smell of mown hay, fresh fields. Davis's socks and the cuffs of his pants were spattered with green pulp which stained his hand when he stooped to brush it away, and then his hand smelled of cut grass. Overhead, in a budding sweet gum tree, a cardinal made his slick whistle, a sound repeated and repeated, "Sex. Sex. Sex. Sex. Sex."

CHAPTER 16

NOT WANTING TO reel in the moment of his funeral home appearance, Davis slackened the line, letting the minutes play out. He had always been a bad fisherman, impatient, certain whatever stream or lake he sat beside or drifted on was empty of everything but water. But now, he felt adept, the consummate angler, knowing exactly what was in Berkley's well-stocked pond.

Taking the long way, he drove through the old black section of town. Almost unchanged since his childhood, the rickety clapboard houses with their warped porches and sagging eaves somehow made a solid neighborhood. Saturday, and the kids were everywhere, playing tag and tossing balls. The smell of cooking flavored the air, turnip greens and corn bread. What would the rest of the menu include? Stewed potatoes and pork shoulder, pinto beans and peach cobbler.

Savoring the meal as he eased to a stop at an intersection where a middle-aged couple waited to cross, he leaned out the window and said, "How're y'all?" No invitation. Not even acknowledgment. And he remembered that he didn't belong here. No one had a chair for him at any table in this part of town. "Move on through the New South, white boy." They didn't say it, but the words seemed articulated by their backs and shoulders as they walked away.

From frame houses to brick, front-yard vegetable gardens to bluegrass lawns, the neighborhoods changed. No tire swings in the oaks, no one walking in the balmy middle of the day. Quiet affluence. Davis wound around until he found the rear of Berkley's, its parking lot clogged, the street double-lined with cars. Nowhere for him to put the Trackless Tank, but he turned into the lot anyway, where several boys chased one another, their feet skittering in gravel. On the rear steps of the building, the predictable group of men loitered with their cigarettes, one of them laughing out a cloud of smoke. Dirty jokes or rumors. Always the same silt swirling at the top, everything slowing and settling in its own time.

The only space for Davis was the space he occupied, in the middle of the driveway, directly opposite the rear door. When he got out and walked up the steps to the entrance, the men stopped their conversation, and one of them said, "S'pose he don't care who he blocks in." Davis turned and studied the man, trying to put a name to the flat face, the thrown-back shoulders. Some second or third cousin. The smokers drew nervously on their cigarettes, a thin haze spiraling above their heads. They were all older than Davis, familiar with death and the civilities of parking. Quick with a brickbat, too, or a two-by-four. Mean to the marrow. That's what his father would say.

"I promise not to park there when I come to your funeral."

No one laughed. The smoke grew thicker, and the flat-faced cousin rocked back and forth on his heels, his hands jammed into his jacket pockets, straining the fabric into bat wings. Davis wondered if he was processing the remark, trying to decide if it was an insult.

"If you gentlemen will excuse me, I've got to go bury my mother." As the door closed behind him, he heard throat-clearing and a jumble of low voices.

The odor of chrysanthemums was overpowering, and organ music seeped from hidden speakers in the ceiling. In the parlor nearest the door, someone was keening. When Davis looked inside, he saw a family clinging to one another in a half circle around a coffin at the far end of the room.

"Young boy, just seventeen. A real shame," Mr. Berkley whispered from somewhere behind him. In the dim light, he was barely visible, propped against the wall between two large floral displays. "Most of your family's here already, Mr. Banks."

Davis interpreted the remark as reproval. He was later than a son should be when his mother has been waiting so patiently. And he was neglecting the people who had come to see how he was taking it, the death of his last parent. So much depended on him. The bereft, unfortunate son.

"How did the boy die?"

"Car wreck. Out on the Dickson Highway. Awful tragedy." Mr. Berkley dropped his head in a prayerful posture as he finished. Then, looking over Davis's left shoulder, he continued, "Sometimes the visitation is worse than the funeral, everyone seeing the deceased for the first time. This will be a hard day."

For a moment, Davis felt he was glimpsing the inner workings of the death business—the two or three or five stages of moving the bodies along. Assembly line. First the crack-up or collapse. Then the makeup and the pose and all that grief to be parceled out in viewings, visitations, burials. Ellen Banks and her family were nearing the end of the line, out the door and into the ground, with a boy to follow and an endless procession of the dead to follow him.

How Mr. Berkley would hate Charles Winningham, who had contrived or provoked his own burial, eliminating the funeral business entirely. Still, he might get Winningham in the end—what was left of him—for proper interment, with all the rites and discreet tally sheets for supplies and services rendered. Sad to think that a man couldn't just lie down in the kindred dust.

As he entered the parlor where his mother was on display, Davis stumbled in awe of the flowers—wreaths and sprays and garlands and arrangements on wire tripods, little pots in colored foil, milky vases jammed with carnations and irises—so many blooms they almost obscured the coffin. His mother would consider this a good showing. She counted a person's worth by the quantity of flowers. Depth of grief measured in gladiolas, tulips, mums, lilies. But there was nothing from him, no white roses tagged with a "Mother" ribbon, blue to match her dress. He should have remembered. But then she knew he never approved of this wastefulness, had withdrawn into silence when he referred to his father's funeral as a horror-show hothouse. He wondered if she had ever forgiven him.

"Thank the Lord, you're finally here." Aunt Goldie sidled up to him, her whisper loud enough for everyone in the back of the room to hear.

She was clutching a program, which Davis tugged from her gloved grasp. "Rock of Ages," "The Old Rugged Cross," all the old Baptist standards. Sermon by Pastor Roy Watkins. "Who's Watkins?" he asked Aunt Goldie.

"That's him, sittin' right down front on the end."

From behind, the man she singled out might be dead himself. He wasn't seated so much as tilted into a folding chair, his legs outthrust, head tipped forward.

"Used to be the pastor down at Blooming Grove. He don't do much preachin' now but knows your uncle Oscar."

"The old-boy-done-been-called-to-preachin' network," Davis thought, wondering if Oscar was building credits with his buddy Roy. Might be a kind of geriatric exchange, with an invitation for Oscar looming in some rural church as payback.

"Testimonials." The word was printed in the middle of the program, immediately before "Sermon." "Whose idea was this?" Davis was bending down to Aunt Goldie, his finger underneath the word.

"Your mama always liked it when friends and family said a few words."

In other words, it was Goldie's idea. She and Oscar had organized the funeral program.

Realizing his aunt was shushing him and turning away, Davis followed and took his seat between her and Pastor Watkins, who did not pull back his legs for them to pass. From his seat, Davis could see the tip of his mother's nose and part of her forehead, her profile held in marble relief. The organist was stammering through "Blessed Assurance" on the little keyboard set up in the corner. Someone behind Davis was humming.

When the music stopped, Oscar stood and moved slowly to the front amid shuffling and coughing. "Praise the Lord," he said, waiting as if he expected the Lord to reply. "It's good to see so many friends here, even on this sad occasion. Ellen Banks was my sister by marriage, and I loved her so good—just like a sister. Her passing is hard for us all, but she's safe in the bosom of Jesus. Praise the Lord." A few people now echoed, "Praise the Lord." "She's gone to a better place."

Oscar sat down so abruptly that Davis thought he might be

ill. Brevity was not his strength. Stammering in circles and going on to no point was his usual style. No one knew what to do next. The program indicated they were at the "Testimonials" section, but no one came forward. Goldie knuckled his thigh, but he didn't want to speak. Didn't the next of kin get a free pass where these things were concerned? The sound of anticipation was a white noise in the room, undertone of all those bodies breathing and shifting in their chairs. Davis stood up.

When he turned to face the room, he realized for the first time how many people had come. Extra chairs had been set up at the back and along the walls. A small group of latecomers stood just inside the door. They were all looking at him, the professor, the skilled public speaker. But he had nothing to say. Casting a glance behind him, he saw his mother waiting. Her last thoughts, the ones decaying in her brain, were probably of Haupt. If he weren't still in the hospital, Haupt might even be in the room.

He was on the brink of saying something absurd, to suit the situation: "My mother's last words were 'cottage cheese.' " The words were forming in his mouth, but what came out instead when he proclaimed her dying expression was "I'm at ease." "The doctor who tried to save her life told me. She was in terrible pain, in and out of consciousness as they worked on her. At the end, she motioned, and when the doctor leaned over she said, 'I'm at ease.' I take comfort in those words, as all of you who knew and loved her should. Ellen Banks is at ease."

Aunt Goldie gave him a perplexed, cocked-head look as he sat down beside her. Almost touching his lips to her ear, Davis whispered, "Cottage cheese."

"What'd you say?"

Davis gave a somber look and turned to sit squarely in his chair. After more shuffling and awkward silence, he leaned to Pastor Watkins and said, "Time for the sermon."

Without answering, the old man went into action, pulling his legs toward him and hoisting himself up like someone balancing on a windblown ledge. His shirt was stained with coffee or tobacco juice, which his off-center necktie couldn't cover. Speaking without notes, nothing but a Bible in his hands, he began.

"Friends, loved ones, children of God, we are here on this sad occasion to mark the passing of Mrs. Banks." A loud moan from the back of the room unsteadied him. "She was a good woman—a daughter, sister, wife, and mother." Coughs rippled through the room, a sign the preacher was slow in warming to his subject. "Helen Banks, a name that will now be engraved on a stone is also written in the Book of Life in Heaven." Someone said, "Praise, Jee-sus!" and the preacher cleared his throat, saying Ellen's name wrong again. "Helen Banks . . ." He wasn't so much lost in thought as simply lost. Davis crossed and uncrossed his legs, wondering how to jump-start the old man so he could finish. The room was a bubble of air sunk in amber. Around them, the moments hardened.

"How do we reckon the passing of a human life?" From nowhere, the preacher had returned. "Can we put a dollar value on it? Can we weigh it in pounds or measure it in inches? No, brothers and sisters, we cannot. And yet each life is precious to God, even the littlest. For His eye is on the sparrow. So we come here on this fine April Saturday to say good-bye to someone we cherished but God values even more. Among the flowers today, I saw one of those arrangements with the little telephone off the hook and the words 'Jesus called' on the ribbon. Yes, my friends, Jesus called Helen Banks and took her home."

The old man stood for a moment, apparently trying to determine if he was through, and then prayed, "Sweet Jesus, we know this good woman is in your care. We pray that if there be any here today who do not know you, who have not taken you as their personal savior, that they will realize how short life is. Lord, let us all be ready. Amen."

"Amen" sounded throughout the room as the preacher walked to his chair and sat heavily next to Davis. The organist began to play, something that at first sounded like "The Girl from Ipanema" but slowed into "Just As I Am." Aunt Goldie was standing, motioning to Davis and Uncle Oscar. She meant for the three of them to form a receiving line at the head of the casket. This was the part Davis hadn't remembered—everyone filing through to view the body, then shake the hands of the grieving family. Aunt Goldie nudged him closest to the body, a director positioning an actor onstage. Then she stood next to him and put Oscar at the end of their short line.

Not everyone who passed by looked at the body, but some stopped and stared briefly. A few of the women even bent and kissed Ellen Banks's forehead or her waxy cheek. The tendered consolations were a background noise, like the public address system in an airport: Sorry for your loss. Your lost baggage. Lost. Sorry. Sorry. Sorry. Some of the older women hugged him or patted the back of his hand. The men gave a stoic look and mumbled. Some said nothing.

Next to him, Aunt Goldie was offering a constant patter, and Davis eventually realized it was an announcement. "Burial's been changed to tomorrow at two." Whatever anyone said to her, that was her reply.

On the periphery, Uncle Oscar occasionally cleared his throat to bellow a big hello at someone he hadn't seen in a long time. When Oscar stopped the flow with his socializing, Davis pulled people along until they pushed the blockage through. "Thank you. Thank you so much for coming. Thanks. Thank you." And then there would be four people moving past Aunt Goldie's announcement of the burial postponement, bumping into Oscar's gab.

Linda was in the line. She stopped to place a single rose inside the coffin and then turned to Davis to ask if he minded. "Hell, yes. Get it out of there. Nobody needs any tokens from you," but he killed the thought and said it was all right. Linda's hand was damp when he shook it. She said nothing but gave him her best compassionate look.

When the crowd had gone and only a few of Aunt Goldie's friends from church waddled around her, making dovecote chatter, Davis went to the back of the room and sat down. Oscar was swapping pulpit tips with Pastor Watkins, who had not moved since giving his sermon. Maybe he was waiting to be paid. What should he get for such an inspirational message, especially one tailored so carefully to fit the deceased? Coin of the realm, Reverend—a fistful of dust.

A few people sauntered in the hallway, but most were outside the funeral home. From the top of the steps, Davis could see that his car had been moved, maybe by the men who disapproved of his parking habits, possibly by Mr. Berkley. Unless it had been towed, it had to be nearby, pushed out of the way. As the lot thinned out, sunlight on glass in the rose of Sharon bushes flashed the location. Rolled completely off the graveled lot and onto a portion of the lawn, the car spoke its wounded word through small-leafed branches—LIER.

·

With all the windows down and the warm air rushing in, Davis swung onto the bypass and watched the speedometer needle rise. The smell of mums still clung to him, and nothing on the radio could drown out Aunt Goldie's repetition: "Burial's been changed to tomorrow at two."

At ease. For the first time, Davis realized what an odd slip it was. Military. How often had his mother been at ease with Haupt? Yes, she might well have said she was at ease or easy. Easy does it. Easy all the way. Let me down easy. Easy street and easy chair. As easy as falling off a building. Easy as pie. Praise the Lord and ease me over to the other side.

His mother had died late Wednesday night, so the rigor might still be in her joints and muscles. But it would slowly let go, ease up, let her relax into death. Such a stern attention she held, mustered into death's camp. Poor recruit. How much he wanted her to be at ease.

CHAPTER 17

SLOWING FROM BYPASS speed, Davis turned in the direction of the cemetery. Funny how every street in Clarksville that doesn't dead-end leads to the dead-end gates of Greenwood. But then, if you were going to Leon's Tap Room, the streets would have the same inevitability. Rome is where the roads lead only if you're going to Rome. Piece it together any way you like, the end justifies the route. No matter how roundabout or wrong, make enough turns and you'll be there.

But Greenwood or someplace like it wasn't a matter of choice. Lie down anywhere you like, and still you'll end up in the ground somewhere. Still. Winningham knew this principle better than anyone. Davis's mother knew it too, having inscribed her name in granite eight years ago. This was the end of every road.

The backhoe was parked and silent. "Too early for the reinterment," Davis thought, reading names and dates in the covering grass. But when he stood at the edge of the open pit, he saw that half of it had been filled, his mother's half, red earth bulging like a wound that wouldn't heal. Checking his smashed watch, Davis wondered how long he had meandered to get here. Had the time warped somehow, causing him to miss her burial? The sun flared between clouds. The name on the mounded side of the grave was his mother's, the death date still uncut in the veined stone.

"They've put my father on the wrong side. Stupid assholes!" He turned around several times, clenching his fists and pulling his arms in hard against his chest. "Jesus Christ Almighty! They didn't even look at the marker."

Uphill, someone wandering among the graves stopped to look at Davis, probably thinking she was looking at grief, the wail of loss, the cry of rage against the unanswering end. Dervish of an ancient ache, he spun beneath the cloud-broken sky.

Thinking only of the coroner and his coveralled drones, Davis aimed himself in the direction of his car and broke into a sprint, tripping on a footstone hidden in the grass. For an instant, he was splayed above the ground like a bad diver and could see the whole of Greenwood, its swells and placid surfaces, the deep green bay at the edge of forever. But when he hit, the vision left in a single exhalation, breath knocked loose in a primitive grunt.

Rising first to his knees, then rocking back with his legs folded under him, Davis took inventory. His ribs ached from the impact; the thumb on his left hand throbbed. No serious damage. But the knees of his pants and his coat sleeves were smeared, grass stains showing as a slickness on the black cloth, clay earth dark in the weave like clotted blood.

The woman watching him had come halfway down the hill and stopped. He waved an embarrassed all-clear, a blackboard erasure motion, as he stumbled to his feet. When he got to the car and sat down, he wasn't so sure about himself. His left arm held a low hum in the elbow and wrist, and his heart was going too fast. Thinking it could be insulin shock, he fumbled with his monitor, pricking three fingers before getting any blood. 142. Not an insulin reaction. Had to be the jolt, the shock of the fall. The anger. "Goddamned coroner!"

.

By the time Davis reached the coroner's office, he had a hammering headache, which intensified when he pushed against the door and found it locked. NO REGULAR WEEKEND HOURS. "Well, how about a few irregular ones? A fucking irregular five minutes." He chewed the words and shook the door so hard a guard appeared down the hallway. "Coroner," Davis shouted into the glass.

The guard wagged his head and said, "Come back Monday," before vanishing around his corner. Deadened by the hallway and the plate-glass door, his voice was barely audible. He could have said, "Kiss my ass." The more Davis considered, the more certain he was the guard had insulted him. Using both hands, he shook the door until his arms gave out.

Uphill, in the parking lot, two cops stood looking at him. They held him in view as he walked up the street and entered the police station. As he started through the room toward Ann Louise's cubicle, a voice said, "Hold on there, buddy. Where you think you're going?"

"I think I'm going to see Detective Wilson. That all right

with you?" He was breathless with irritation, barely able to keep from screaming.

"She know you're coming?"

"Why don't you announce me?"

Too far. Davis had pushed him too far. The officer was moving, gesturing toward a bench backed against the outside wall. "Sit down right there, sir." His voice had taken on a spooky formality. "Identification, please, sir."

Davis leaned forward, fumbling for his wallet. Looking at the Iowa driver's license and then at Davis, the officer said, "You been in an accident?"

"Look, I just came to see Ann Louise Wilson. If you'll tell her I'm here, you can get back to something really important, like your doughnuts." Why couldn't he stop his mouth? This confrontation wasn't one he wanted. Self-important people. He hated them all. No reason to single this one out on this day of all days.

"Just sit where you are, sir." The officer kept the license and walked back to his seat at the window counter. Clacking at his computer, he looked from the keyboard to Davis, holding him in place. When he finally said, "I'll see if Detective Wilson is here," Davis figured he hadn't turned up on any of the most-wanted lists.

Ann Louise appeared at the doorway and motioned Davis to follow her. When they reached her desk, she handed him his license and said, "What'd you do to piss Walter off? He's ready to put you in one of our guest rooms." Then, noticing his smeared clothing, "What happened to you?"

"Why didn't you wait for me when you buried my father?"

"You were pretty upset this morning. I figured all that mattered was getting your father back in his grave as quickly as possible."

"You put my father on the wrong side of the grave, where

my mother was supposed to go." Davis could tell that Ann Louise was visualizing the grave site. As she slowly understood, the set expression on her face smoothed into disbelief.

"Weren't you there?" Davis tipped his head to one side.

"If I had been, do you think I would have screwed up like that?"

"So it was the coroner."

"Probably one of his assistants. Ted's in Nashville for the weekend at a forensics seminar."

"How am I supposed to know my father's in the grave at all?"

"Where else would he be?"

"All I know is, I didn't get to see my father put back in his coffin, and now something's buried where my mother ought to be. Maybe Ted and his colleagues are using him for a specimen centerpiece down at the Opryland Hotel."

"Okay, I understand. You're mad as hell. I would be too."

"This is no joke, Detective. If my father is in that hole, he's on the wrong side. How am I ever gonna know he's there at all, except on somebody's say-so?"

"If you're suggesting we dig him up again, we'll need another exhumation order. Won't be able to until Monday. How long do you want to wait to bury your mother?"

Davis hadn't forgotten about his mother, stalled at Berkley's, pushed to a back room in the old house. She should have been in the ground today. Waiting another three or four days would be obscene, a desecration. "Burial's scheduled for two o'clock tomorrow."

"Okay. Follow through with that and then we'll need an order to exhume your mother when we switch the coffins around. Believe me, Davis, this stuff gets complicated in a hurry."

"Then we'll have to put her on the wrong side too. Names on the stone won't match with the bodies."

Ann Louise pushed away from her desk and rolled her chair closer to Davis. "I'm truly sorry. And I know this is a hard enough time for you. But God will know who's who."

"Bury 'em and let God sort 'em out. Where've I heard that before?"

Drawing back, Ann Louise let her hands drop into her lap. "It's your call. I'll do whatever you want done."

For the first time since falling at Greenwood, Davis felt his pulse slow. "Man, I've got such a headache."

Ann Louise rattled a bottle of something from one of her desk drawers and handed it to Davis with her half-finished cup of coffee.

He shook out two tablets and took a sip, then finished the lukewarm coffee in a single gulp, eyeing the sugar residue at the bottom.

"Oh, my God! There was sugar in it!" She tipped toward him, one hand clasping the other, a look of terror on her face.

"It's okay. Everything evens out in the end." He was thinking of the big end, with a capital "E," but let Ann Louise assume he was talking about blood sugar levels.

"Could you eat?"

The question was so elliptical and out of context that Davis didn't get it.

When he didn't answer, Ann Louise added, "Would you like to go somewhere for a bite, if it doesn't complicate your diabetes, I mean?"

Davis knew he should eat. If he got the food and the insulin just right, maybe the pain in his head would untwist; maybe the hopelessness lowering over him like a coffin lid would lift.

Ann Louise took him to the Pic-a-Rib. "Best barbecue in town. You do like barbecue, don't you?" They had just parked, and Ann Louise kept her hand on the keys in the ignition, ready to leave if Davis objected.

Davis said, "Sure," but was calculating the molasses and brown sugar in the sauce, how much insulin he would need. He never estimated this kind of meal well, always under or over, always high or low two hours after eating. Ann Louise seemed so pleased with her choice of restaurants that he hid his concern. "Haven't had good barbecue in years."

After they were seated and had placed their orders, Davis went to the bathroom to take his injection. Familiar territory, this sloppy public space, smelling of urine and disinfectant. Over the years, he had perfected the process—washing his hands and bumping the stall door open, then closed, with his hip. Inside, he took the syringe and the insulin from his pocket and drew up what he guessed he would need. One quick jab and it was done. Not exactly antiseptic conditions, but not bad, considering.

The food was slow in coming, and Davis became more distracted as he thought of the insulin spreading through his bloodstream with no sugar to uptake. When the meal finally arrived, he ate too quickly. Ann Louise was half through when he pushed his empty plate aside.

"Does that mean you liked it?" she asked, touching the corners of her mouth with her napkin.

"It was great." In truth, Davis hadn't tasted much. All that mattered was overtaking the insulin with food. "Sorry I ate so fast. Habit of living alone," he lied.

"I think I eat less since Buford and I divorced. Meals just aren't a big thing when there's nobody else there."

The name caused Davis to lift his hand to his throat. Buford could be watching them now. "Did you two come here often?"

"We didn't eat out much. Buford's idea of a good meal was a bucket of chicken and a quart of Pepsi."

"So, food drove you apart?"

"Honest answer? He always thought I was playing around on him."

"And were you?"

Ann Louise lifted a spoon and stirred slowly in her little bowl of baked beans. "Yeah, me and Robert Redford."

Her answer was evasive, which could mean yes or that she wanted Davis to think it could be yes. Odd to be flirting, considering how far they had already gone together. Almost gone.

"You ever cheat on Linda?"

"Well, that's a whole 'nother story, as they say hereabouts. Linda and I worked out for about seventy-two hours. After that, it was every spouse for him- or herself."

"What was the problem?"

The word "problem" made Davis wince. But then why wouldn't she wonder, after his nonperformance last night? "Mostly, we were too young. Didn't know what we were getting into. She wanted kids and I didn't." There it was again, suggestion of sexual dysfunction. "It wasn't the diabetes. I didn't become diabetic until after we divorced."

"Didn't you love each other?"

"Didn't you and Buford?"

Acknowledging their stalemate, Ann Louise folded her paper napkin into a small square and said, "All done."

"Do you really like living where you grew up, right here in Clarksville?" Davis asked the question as they wandered through the parking lot, trying to spot Ann Louise's car.

"Actually, I grew up in New Providence, but it got swallowed up by Clarksville years ago. This town is my home. What else can I tell you?"

"Feels like another world to me. When I'm in Des Moines and I think about this place, it doesn't seem real. Feels like someone else grew up here and told me about it. Remember Tiny Faust, wore men's clothes and walked down the middle of the street, always had that little dog with her? Cars just looped around, because that was Tiny. Nothing you could do about her. See how much that sounds like a story, like something made up? It's hard to come back to an unreal place."

"So what does it feel like when you're here?"

They were sitting in the car in the Pic-a-Rib parking lot. Ann Louise had started the engine but hadn't put the shift into drive. "Feels exactly like this, idling because there's nowhere to go." The analogy wasn't quite right, but Davis let it stand.

"I don't get it. Clarksville's a decent enough town, and I've seen the worst parts of it, believe me."

"Guess you'll live here until they shovel you under in Greenwood."

"I prefer Riverview." As she named the other cemetery, she laughed and eased the car onto the street. "Guess we should get you home."

This was the moment of impasse, the kind Davis remembered from high school when he mapped out the evening like a battle campaign, shaping everything to end in a kiss. Was she hinting at an invitation? What if he suggested her place instead? How could things have changed so little after all the years? He needed a foolproof way to extend the evening.

"Tell you what. You give me a tour of your hometown, and I'll give you one of mine. How's that?"

Ann Louise thought for a moment, then made a quick U-turn. "First stop's the old neighborhood."

"New Providence, you mean."

"Don't try to outguess the driver, just sit back and enjoy the sights."

She toured him past a succession of comfortable houses, all with big yards and old trees, places where she was five or eight or seventeen. Some of the schools were ones she and Davis had in common, where they had known of, if not known, each other. There once stood the malt stand that served the best root-beer floats on earth, the drive-in theater where she sneaked in to see *A Summer Place*. A carpet store covered the place where she had learned to swim. She took Davis down the street where her father had taught her how to drive and to a field where she remembered flying kites.

Not a bad memory in the trip. No illness or death. Not a word of Buford or any other boy or man. Her Clarksville was pristine because it no longer existed. Maybe Davis's was ruined for the same reason. Time to find out. Ann Louise agreed to let him get behind the wheel.

CHAPTER 18

DARKNESS SMOOTHED AND tucked itself in place as Davis steered down streets pinched tight with pickups and cars jacked up in the rear like sprinters in their starting blocks. A wrong turn took him through a trailer park as bleak as an inner-city neighborhood, aluminum walls sprayed with gang signs and obscenities, broken windows holding the moon's reflection in jagged teeth. No outlet. But even when he turned around and started back through, Ann Louise was calm.

"Need directions?" she needled.

"Hey, it's been a while, okay?"

Traffic on the Fort Campbell Highway was heavy. Saturday night. Date night. Time to get drunk, get a little crazy. Davis had to force a place for himself in the solid line of cars and then turned off almost immediately into the parking lot of the Vacation Motor Lodge.

"This place was here when we were kids. Remember? I used to wish I knew someone who would let me swim in the pool. Didn't know my father might be spending some quality time with Charles Winningham in one of the rooms."

"For Christ's sake, Davis!"

"Hey, it's just one version, not the one I was working with all these years, but it works for you, doesn't it? Might also be the place where my mother was screwing"—he almost said Haupt—"God knows who. That's a version."

Ann Louise let out a sulky sigh. "Come on, Davis. Life isn't versions or options."

Shutting off the engine and leaning back into the yellow glow of the VACANCY sign, Davis said, "Go ahead and run with that idea."

"Things happen or they don't happen. The facts are the facts." Ann Louise locked her arms across her chest and looked straight ahead.

"Do you know for a fact that my father knew Charles Winningham?"

"Let's just say the evidence points strongly in that direction."

"Now, wait. Wouldn't it be more accurate to say the interpretation bends that way?"

"I'm a cop. Following leads and going where they take me is my job."

"Suppose I could prove to you, beyond a reasonable doubt, that Ralph Banks and Charles Winningham never heard of each other. How would that fit with your trail of leads?"

"But you can't prove it."

"Just suppose I could."

"Why not suppose you could prove your father was Babe Ruth?"

Davis started the engine, muttering "Shit" as he dodged back into traffic. "You could at least admit you're not sure."

"Neither are you, or you wouldn't be playing this game."

"Then you admit you're not sure."

Ann Louise took in a deep breath as if to make a long statement, then exhaled slowly. They were wedged in traffic, pulled along at the speed of the highway current. "Somewhere, under everything else, something happened. We can't always know for one-hundred-percent certain what it was, but we can get close. It's what I do."

Davis felt at home as he listened to Ann Louise. Safe ground for someone accustomed to playing with the interpretation of texts. "Suppose two cars wreck at a busy intersection. Twenty people witness it. When the cops take statements, how many versions of the accident will they get?"

"Oh, a story problem! Haven't heard one of those since ninth grade. Don't you really want to know how far apart the cars will be when they're towed away in opposite directions?"

"Just answer the question. Will all twenty people tell the same story?"

"No."

"Is it possible that some of the witnesses will blame one driver and some the other?"

"This is tiresome, Davis. You already know what the answers are."

"Okay, then just substitute Winningham and my father for the two drivers. They somehow collided at Greenwood Cemetery. No eyewitnesses. Everybody comes along later to view the scene. How do we know which of the stories they tell is the right one?"

"Something happened. Winningham was under your father's coffin. That's a fact."

"But how and why did he get there? That's where all the interpretation begins."

Warming to the game, Ann Louise returned to Davis's hypothetical wreck. "We wouldn't just rely on witness statements, you know. We'd measure skid marks. Look for point of impact. Inspect damage to both cars. The evidence would lead us to a particular conclusion."

"In other words, you'd figure out a logical way to tell the story of the wreck."

"Figuring it out isn't the same thing as making it up."

"Do the skid marks and bent fenders always tell an obvious story?"

"Combined with all those conflicting witness statements and common sense, they generally do."

"What if one of the drivers is a little old lady? Any chance her age might cause an officer to jump to conclusions about her driving ability?"

"There's no end to this game, is there?"

"You're giving up, then?"

"I'm getting tired. Cover them with as much dirt or as many versions as you like, but facts are facts."

"What I'm after is the way we come to know the facts. Lots of room there for versions, don't you think?"

Ann Louise looked out her side window and said nothing. The traffic thinned out at Riverside Drive when Davis kept going uphill into the heart of Clarksville. "Bet you were born over there in the old hospital." Davis's right hand fluttered off the wheel and back, giving the smallest sign of direction, getting no response.

Ann Louise might have thought Davis was headed for the police station and his own car, but when he passed the turnoff, she said nothing until he zagged through an older section of town and pulled to the curb. Rambling two-story frame houses lined both sides of the street. The kind of neighborhood that might eventually be gentrified or yuppified. "What're we doing here?"

"Thought you might like to see where I was born." Davis pointed to a weathered white house with a wraparound porch. "Right there."

"Your mother didn't make it to the hospital in time?"

"She planned to have me at home. Wasn't a believer in doctors. A neighbor stood in as midwife and took care of everything. My father took the afterbirth and buried it in the side yard. It was June, hot as blazes, and he dug a little grave and shoveled it under." In the streetlight, Davis could see the solemn expression on Ann Louise's face as she visualized the process.

"Something I never told a soul," he continued, eyes fixed on the house, "is I've always thought they buried my twin there."

Ann Louise studied the house in silence.

"If I ever have enough money, I'm going to buy the old place and have the yard dug up."

"Why do you think you were a twin?"

"I've always felt part of me is missing. Feeling's been even stronger since I became diabetic. The big clue is that I was never given a middle name. Or maybe Davis is a middle name and I don't have a first one. I think my parents picked out a girl's name and a boy's. When two boys came, they split the boy's names between my twin and me. Maybe he was William."

"Pretty flimsy evidence."

"My grandmother had a twin. Olivia and Viola. My mother said you couldn't tell them apart. They'd sometimes trade places to see how long it would take someone to notice. Sometimes I dream of my stillborn brother. Other times, he's alive when my father shovels the dirt over his face. My folks never had much money. Must have been a jolt to have two babies."

Shaken by the story and its grisly possibilities, Ann Louise said, "Twins don't always both survive."

"But why me and not him? Or what if I am him? What if it was me who died that day?" Watching Ann Louise's face grow more serious, more concerned, Davis continued, "What if none of this is true?"

Rising from her webby reverie, Ann Louise demanded, "What's not true?"

Davis just looked at her, his face impassive.

"You mean none of what you just told me is true? Is that what you mean?"

"I didn't say that."

"Then what the hell did you say?"

"I said what if none of this is true."

"In other words, you're still playing the game, the goddamned stupid game! Well, to hell with you, Davis Banks."

"Hold on. Hold on. What'd I do?"

"You made up the whole story, didn't you? Every bit of it was a lie."

"I never said that."

"It is a lie, isn't it?"

"I just offered up a big chunk of my soul to you and you think I was lying? So much for your detective's intuition."

"Were you lying, Davis? Tell me honestly. Were you?"

"Why not just follow the leads and figure it out for yourself?"

For a moment, Davis thought Ann Louise would strike him. Then she fumbled her seat belt off and opened the door.

When she crossed the street and stood looking at the house, where no lights showed from inside, Davis wondered if she might start digging in the yard. Pacing the sidewalk, she seemed agitated enough to scoop the earth with her bare hands. When she returned to the car, she stood rigidly at the driver's door and said, "Get out."

Davis did as he was told, stumbling into the middle of the street as Ann Louise drove away, her brake lights winking once at the top of the hill, nothing left but the slight chill of the air. He could walk the half mile to the parking lot to get his car. Ann Louise must have calculated the nearness before she left him. Wouldn't have dumped him if they had been miles into nowhere. Or would she? How was she already shaping the story that would explain herself to herself—the one that would explain him?

Walking along Second Street, Davis felt invisible, not airy but dense, a black hole, a shadow like a blink. He was present only in the moment when the lids went down. Gone when they went up again. By the time he got to the car, he was a blotch on the window, a thick smudge on glass. Someone driving by was playing loud music, bass notes rumbling in Davis's stomach, a steady throbbing, like a second pulse. Heartbeat of the person he never was, the twin he might have been. Spun in a gauzy fatigue, he lay across the front seat, face pressed into the ribbed cushion, hands twitching an abstract sleep-language.

•

The silence woke him, and at first he thought he was dreaming. The parking lot lights hovered orange-white around him, the only noise his own throat trying to swallow. "Time." The thought was a movement in his left arm, bringing his wrist near his face. Broken time. No time. Alarm for high blood sugar far away in his head, like the muffled thud of underground pounding.

He started the engine and pulled into the abandoned street, the rumble of the exhaust loud against the buildings. Stoplights flashed their between-time yellow. Even the drunks had long ago staggered to their hidden corners. Rolling down his window, letting the cool air pour in, Davis felt part of something big and calm and secure. Emptiness. Obscurity. The heaviness in his bones was the packed-down heaviness of earth. A burial and a resurrection.

Nearing his mother's house, he shut off the engine and coasted the last half block, making a sharp turn into the driveway. Silence of the dead and the come-again. Home. He silently rounded the word, letting it fill his mouth, feeling it end in a little kiss. A peck on the cheek of the vanishing moment. This time it seemed right not to find his mother there, his mind already making the erasures.

In his old bedroom he pulled his father's suits from the closet and tugged armloads of his mother's dresses from the drooping line, piling them near the front door. Next came record albums, boxes of photographs, and the croquet mallet with black rings, the one his father always chose. From his mother's bedroom, he took only the companion pillow.

Davis thought of tomb rummagers hauling out everything sacred to some pharoah. But this was more like a garage-sale pile, a dump for Goodwill. No one else would want these things. But he needed something to show for the years, parts of the past to hold his version of the past in place. Stuffing the trunk and then the backseat, cramming hard and shouldering for greater compaction, he filled the car. When he thought he couldn't get anything else in, he went back for more and pushed harder. No matter if everything was jumbled and crumpled, it could be sorted later, smoothed out like the telling of a story, or not smoothed but still a story in itself. Ralph and Ellen and Davis. As simple as that.

When nothing else would fit except the pictures hanging on the living room wall, Davis phoned Ann Louise.

After nine rings, Ann Louise's voice answered with a hoarse "This better be good."

"Should I sell the house or burn it?"

"This some kind of sick joke?"

"I'm trying to decide how to manage my mother's estate, and my options are to sell her house or burn it. Which do you think I should do?"

"Davis? I think you need to sober up."

"Haven't had a drop. You gonna give me your opinion or not?"

"Couldn't this have waited until morning?"

Davis responded by hanging up the phone. On his way out the door, he thought of the videocassette that had been recording when he arrived from the airport and stopped to eject it from the machine. He remembered the Brenda Lee album tipped against the wall at the end of the sofa and took it too. Then he stepped onto the front porch, looked back inside one last time, and left the door standing open. "To let the night in," he thought.

When he stopped for gas at an all-night station, the man in the little booth said, "Now that's the way to pack a car."

Something about his drawl, the slow way he said the word "car," made Davis laugh, and then he couldn't stop. What a great joke everything was. How infinitely funny.

"Take an IOU?" he asked through his laughter.

The drawling man grinned uncertainly, not understanding the humor.

"Oh, hell. Just put it on my tab. William Banks. Charge it

to William Davis Banks," Davis said, getting behind the wheel as the attendant rushed out of the booth yelling for him to stop. Knowing the man would call the police, Davis doubled back toward Clarksville and took the first rural road that led in the direction of the interstate. The car's rumble leveled out as he drove faster, and soon he was seeing the signs for I-24.

"East or west?" he thought. "East or west." Then, simply because the east ramp came first, he turned onto it and headed in the direction of Nashville. "Gonna be a country music star. Yahoo!" he yelled, reaching for the radio dial. But as he neared the last Clarksville exit, he slowed and took it, stopping at the end of the ramp. How could he have forgotten his mother, his unburied mother in her blue dress? What if no one but Goldie and Oscar and Pastor Watkins came for the service, the three of them scraping the soft earth from their shoes and talking of the bosom of the Good Lord?

As he sat beneath the wheeling sky, musty scent of old clothing blooming in the car, sachet of dead petals, the blue light of a patrol cruiser strobed behind him. He shifted upright and sat motionless as the officer adjusted his spotlight so that it illuminated the car. Davis watched in the mirror as the figure approached, hand on his gun.

When the cop got near enough to bend down and look in the window, he said, "Davis? Davis Banks?" It was Earl Hearndon, a high school classmate. "What are you doing out here in the middle of the night?"

"I was just trying to get home."

"You got gas without paying back there at the all-night station."

"Did I?"

Earl stood up and reflected for a moment, then bent down close to the window. "Sorry to hear about your mama. Haven't been drinking, have you, Davis?"

Davis huffed a deep breath in Earl's direction.

"What the hell is all this stuff?" Earl was shining his flashlight inside, illuminating blouses and pants and socks.

"Laundry."

"Look, I'll take care of that gas bill, but you've got to follow me. I'll get you home. Okay?"

Davis nodded and waited for Earl to get back into his squad car and pull around him. His blue lights drew Davis back from the outskirts of town and into the neighborhood where his mother had lived. When they reached her house, Earl pulled over and let Davis arc around him into the driveway.

All the lights were on, and Ann Louise was standing in the doorway. When she stepped onto the porch, the beam from behind was an incline she descended. Davis felt the old bone-weariness, sweet fatigue of coming home, sugar tide risen in the blood. When he leaned back and closed his eyes, he was deep in the crystalized thicket, but someone was coming nearer; someone was calling his name.

ABOUT THE AUTHOR

NEAL BOWERS was born and raised in Clarksville, Tennessee, but has lived the past quarter century in Ames, Iowa. Among his six previous books, the most recent are *Words for the Taking: The Hunt for a Plagiarist* (nonfiction) and *Night Vision* (poetry). He and his wife, Nancy, also a writer, are supervised by six very helpful cats.

ABOUT THE TYPE

This book was set in Simoncini Garamond, a typeface designed by Francesco Simoncini based on the style of Garamond that was created by the French printer Jean Jannon after the original models of Claude Garamond.